A NEW NORMAL LIFE

Her marriage ended. Her story didn't.

Deborah Kedzierski

To everyone who has had to adjust to a new normal life. I hope you had friends and family to bring light to your dark days.

CONTENTS

PROLOGUE

I had to be there by 10 a.m.

I'd set my alarm a little later than usual, but it didn't really matter. I don't think I slept at all. But honestly, I had not slept well in months, maybe longer. There seemed to always be something on my mind.

By 7, I gave up. I padded downstairs to my sister's kitchen for coffee. I'd moved in with her and my 13-year-old nephew, Mattie, a few months ago, after my husband and I agreed to go our separate ways.

I chose a suit to wear. Told myself it was for court. I would look professional and put together. Really, I just needed something that made me feel like I wouldn't fall apart.

The weather was gentle, typical of early spring in North Texas. A little chill in the air when I stepped outside, but it would warm into the 60s by afternoon.

It was the kind of day that hinted at something new—fresh starts, open windows, everything in bloom.

And somehow, that made it worse.

How could the world carry on like nothing had happened?

How could the sun shine-today of all days-when everything I had known will be forever changed.

The traffic toward Denton was light. I felt a pang of sympathy for the people heading south toward Dallas or Fort Worth—bumper to bumper already.

I arrived at the courthouse earlier than expected and found a parking spot easily. I'd been here a few times before for jury duty, though I'd never actually served.

I sat in the car, staring at the building, wondering how it had come to this. We loved each other so much in the beginning. Supposedly, we still did. I just couldn't feel it from him. I couldn't say I felt loved. When did that change? When did it stop being enough? Was there something I could have done differently? Could I have compromised any more? God, these words-change and compromise-had become my nemesis over the last few years. Why did things have to change at all when they were so good once. How much of myself did I have to give up to be worthy?

I wondered if *he* would show. He'd signed the papers, agreeing to everything. He didn't *have* to be here. But still—I wondered. Would he come anyway? Would he choose me, choose us, before it was too late?

But I knew better. He'd made his choice in a million subtle ways already.

I steeled myself, grabbed my bag, and headed inside.

The security guard at the door gave me a kind smile as I passed through the metal detector. "Have a good day," she said.

I nodded, managing a faint smile in return.

The courthouse lobby was cavernous, sound echoing off veined marble floors and stone walls. A large brass seal was embedded in the floor at the base of a sweeping staircase. Hallways stretched to the left and right like open arms. I climbed to the third floor where the district courts were and found Courtroom B.

As I entered the room, I was struck by this feeling that the air in the room was somehow different-more still, thicker. Every breath felt like I was pulling it through a straw. All the noise from the hallways and lobby vanished behind me, like someone had pressed mute. It felt like time was standing still.

I took a seat halfway back, near the aisle. I'd never been in a courtroom before. It was smaller than I imagined—intimate, almost. Just five rows of benches for observers. Two small tables sat in front of the railing, each with two chairs. The judge's bench wasn't in the center. Instead, it was U-shaped, with the judge seated to the left, a nameplate marking her place. There were computer monitors at every seat, even the judge's. I found that strangely out of place.

A young couple breezed in, the clattering of the door opening an abrupt disruption in the cloying quiet. They chatted like old friends, at ease in a way that seemed misplaced, considering where we were. Maybe one of them was a client, the other their lawyer. They sat up front, close together.

As the minutes ticked away, I contemplated leaving. I could have just gotten up and walked out. I could have stopped it. He told me the ball was in my court. I could tell him I changed my mind-agreed to his demands for reconciliation.

If he'd done anything, just one thing, to meet me part of the way. But he didn't. Instead, he just said "File. I'm done."

At exactly 10:00 a.m., a bailiff stepped through a door behind the bench.

"All rise! The Texas 342nd District Court is now in session. The Honorable Judge Tanya McPherson presiding."

We stood as the judge entered, flanked by two other people. One sat beside her; the other took the spot at the court reporter's desk. Then we were directed to be seated.

The judge's presence made me suddenly nervous. My knee bounced, and I twisted the ring on my right hand over and over. It was a Mother's Day gift from the kids a few years ago—four birthstones in a row: theirs in the center, mine and their father's on each end. A little band of who we were, all together.

The bailiff called the young couple's case. They walked up, and I could see the bailiff swear both of them in. They exchanged a few words with the judge. I couldn't hear what was said. Moments later, they walked out smiling, just as relaxed as they had been coming in.

Then: "The following case is now before the court—Case #DR22-8654. In the matter of the dissolution of marriage between Timothy Edward Masters and Renee Millicent Masters. Would the parties please approach the bench."

I stood. My legs felt heavy. I walked to the front, toward the bench. The judge didn't look up. I wondered how many times a day she was called to dissolve a marriage. She must be numb to the tears and pained expressions.

The bailiff reached over the bench with a bible in his hand. I touched the bible, and in a cruel twist, remembered the last time I did — *we* did — promising forever.

"Do you swear to tell the truth, the whole truth, and nothing but the truth?"

"I do." I said, and moved to stand before the judge.

"I'm going to ask you a few quick questions, and then you'll be on your way. Please state your full name."

My mouth was dry. My eyes brimmed with tears. I don't think I was even breathing.

"Renee Millicent Masters," I whispered, voice shaky.

The judge looked up sharply. Her expression softened. There was empathy in her eyes—real empathy. She held my gaze as she asked the remaining questions. Her voice was calm and gentle. Professional, but kind. She continued with her questions, and I responded to each speaking as little as possible.

"You have no reasonable expectation for reconciliation?" she asked.

I hesitated. I had sworn to tell the truth. For the first time, I finally accepted the truth.

"No, Your Honor".

She continued with a few more questions, then she signed the documents in front of her and handed them to me.

"Ms. Masters, take these down to the clerk on the first floor—just to the right when you come down the stairs. They'll file them and give you a copy."

I reached for the papers.

She paused. "Good luck to you, Ms. Masters."

No one tells you how quiet endings are.

The beginning is months of planning and parties, culminating in the grandest celebration of all.

The end is a few simple questions, and a signature. Only minutes.

I stared down at the papers as I waited in line at the clerk's office. I had no words.

What was left to say?

I had no tears left. I left them in that courtroom.

I headed for the exit feeling like I was missing a piece of myself. But I wasn't even sure what that piece *was*.

I walked in a wife. A part of a couple, a marriage.

I was walking out...something else.

I just didn't know what yet.

A few minutes later, I stepped outside. The sun was still shining, the sky still blue.

The world hadn't changed.

But I had.

I was alone.

CHAPTER 1

I walked out of the courthouse and spotted a bench nearby. I sat down, needing a minute to process what had just happened.

I was having all kinds of feelings all at once-sadness, relief, confusion, loss. Like an emotional smoothie-blended, chaotic and maybe a little too much spinach.

There really should be a guidebook for the recently—*and I mean very recently*—divorced. Something like: *"So You Just Lost a Husband: Now What?"*

Maybe I should call someone.

I didn't really feel like talking-I didn't want to be that friend. The kind that ruins a perfectly good Tuesday with today's episode of Law and Order: Divorce Addition.

I definitely don't want to call the kids. Even adult children get bruised in a divorce.

Should I call my ex-husband?

Holy crap—I *have* an ex-husband.

I'm someone's *ex-wife* now.

Wow.

That wasn't exactly on my childhood vision board. I wanted to be a teacher, a ballerina, maybe a nun. Never once thought, "You know what would be fun? Divorce court before lunch."

When did I have to change my social media relationship status? Is there a waiting period? Do I just slide over to "Single," or is "It's complicated" a required layover?

Do I have to make an announcement? Should there be cake? A registry? "Newly divorced and accepting Target gift cards."

Maybe something more like a marital obituary?
"Renee Masters, beloved wife of twenty-plus years, passed peacefully from matrimony this morning at 10:17 a.m., survived by her Honda Accord and impressive shoe collection."

Maybe I should've sent *Save the Date* cards for the hearing.
Color scheme: soft gray and mild despair.
Matching tissues and pens for signing the paperwork.

I was deep in this mental Pinterest board of post-divorce stationery when a man walked out of the courthouse and dropped onto the bench beside me. He let out a long, weary sigh and slumped forward.

"Hi," he said, offering me a wan smile.

I'd never really understood what a *wan smile* was—until I realized I was wearing one. It's the smile you fake when your feelings are on strike, especially the happy ones.

I gave him a matching one.

"Hi."

"Rough morning?" he asked.

"Final divorce hearing."

"I'm really sorry to hear that," he said, with genuine sympathy.

"Thanks." I meant it. Somehow, kindness from a stranger felt better than pity from someone I knew.

I figured I should return the favor. "What brings you here?"

"Mediation," he said with a groan. "But we finally reached an agreement. Yeah!" He gave a mock cheer. "It only cost me the cappuccino maker. But I get more time with my son now, so—

totally worth it."

"How old is your son?"

"He'll be 10 in May."

"Well... congratulations?"

Was that the right response to losing a coffee maker but gaining visitation?

"Or... good for you? I don't know what to say."

He laughed. "It's okay. I'm just glad it's done. Now we can both move on."

Move on. Right.

I stood up to leave.

"Hey—I'm David, by the way."

I nodded. "Enjoy the rest of your day, David."

"You too." Another sad smile.

It was a little comforting to realize I wasn't the only person dealing with marital fallout. For weeks, I'd felt like the universe had singled me out-like I was the only one who'd ever sat on the edge of a bed and wondered how love turned into...this.

But standing outside the courthouse, seeing other people—some sad, some relieved, some just tired—it hit me: this happens all the time. Every day, at courthouses just like this one, people untangle lives they once vowed to share forever.

I wasn't alone.

It's easy to sink into the belief that your pain is uniquely awful, and declare yourself the Most Emotionally Wrecked Person on Earth. But the truth is, heartbreak is painfully ordinary. Universal, even.

With that sad perspective, I left for my car.

I had only made it a few steps, when a terrifying thought hit me: I'd just had a conversation with a stranger *outside a courthouse.*

A courthouse, where people get divorced... but also where *criminals* roam. Real ones. Serial killers. Embezzlers. People who don't return shopping carts.

And there I was, chatting it up like we were old friends at Target.

Is this what happens after divorce? Do you lose your sense of self-preservation along with your monogrammed towels? Did I unknowingly sign away my common sense in the divorce settlement—right between the air fryer and the Hulu login?

My mother would be horrified. She taught me better than this. She watches *Dateline.*

For all I knew, he could've really been one of those criminals.

I picked up the pace, grateful I was wearing flats. My "quick pace" turned into an all-out run as I imagined unexpected audits, or a knife in my back. I glanced over my shoulder—no one. Then again, he could be *ducking behind cars.* You never know. Embezzlers were known to be very clever.

I hit the unlock button on my key fob and reached for the first door I could grab—the back door. I dove in, slammed it shut, and hit the lock button. I heard the locks engage, then disengage.

I hit the lock button again. Again the locks engaged, then disengaged.

I mashed the button several times

Locked.

Unlocked.

Locked.

Unlocked again.

Then it hit me: the locks wouldn't stay engaged unless I was in the driver's seat-some new child-safety feature, which would have been extremely helpful about 21 years ago when I'd locked my baby and my keys in the car at daycare drop-off. Twice.

I peered around the parking lot—still no sign of the Court House Killer/Embezzler —but I stayed on high alert. I had to get into the driver's seat. Fast.

One hand on each front seat, I tried to hoist my leg over. My left foot got stuck in the steering wheel. I stood on my tiptoes, twisting and softly cursing.

OK—maybe not softly.

How did we do this in college? We used to crawl into the back seat all the time like it was an Olympic sport. And I was a gold medalist back then. Maybe love—and a flood of hormones —makes you more flexible. Now? I felt like a retired athlete watching reruns of the big game with an ice pack and Bengay.

Still no sign of the Court House Killer/embezzler.

Take two. I sat on the center console and swiveled, dropping one leg into the driver's seat, then the other.

I was mid-hoist into the front seat when I saw movement in the car next to me and heard a knock on my window.

A woman was peering in the driver's window with a look of concern.

"Are you okay? Should I call 9-1-1? I know CPR!"

"I'm fine. Thank you!" I chirped, trying to smile like I wasn't giving a yoga class in my Honda Accord.

She smiled, gave a little shake of her head, and walked off.

Eventually, I got into the driver's seat, adjusted the power seat, locked the doors—and this time, the locks *stayed* locked. I exhaled. I was safe. Probably.

Still, I glanced in the rear-view mirror one last time, just to be sure.

I made it to the exit and was waiting for traffic when I heard a horn.

David? Dylan? Darren? —what did he say his name was?-was in a car beside me, waving. He motioned for me to roll down my window. Either that or he was dancing. Hard to say.

I rolled it down, just in case. Maybe I left my gas cap off again.

"Hey! I noticed you run," he said. "I go to a running group on Wednesdays. We meet at Moonwinks off the square. Three miles. Super casual. You should come!"

"Will do. Thanks," I said, though I was more of a *mall walker* than a runner. Preferably in air conditioning. Preferably near a shoe sale.

He waved and turned right.

I waved, rolled up my window, and headed to the office.

CHAPTER 2

The divorce final, I continued my post-separation routine - sleep, work, mope, cry, repeat. My nephew would often interrupt the critical mope and cry time by having me watch a movie or play a game with him. I honestly don't know how I could've made it without him.

I'd been staying with my sister for about 6 weeks when I started to feel like it was time to find a place of my own. I was moping and crying less and less each day. It was great having my sister's support while I worked out the marriage and divorce. But I was starting to miss my own things. I called Sharon, a longtime family friend and Realtor, and told her I was ready to find a house.

Sharon had been a dear friend of my mother's for as many years as I could count. She'd been married four times. Two ended in divorce, and the last two in death. My Mom told me that Sharon's last husband died in "the throes of passion." I don't know if that is true, but knowing Sharon, I don't doubt it. Sharon was a force of nature. She always lived life to the fullest. She lit up a room when she walked in. I wanted to be Sharon someday. No matter what happened, her glass was never half full; it was overflowing.

"Hey Renee. Your mom told me about your divorce." she said sweetly." I sure am sorry sweetie."

"Thank you." I knew Sharon had always liked my ex-husband. He and her third husband used to play golf together. "I don't want you to feel like you can't still be friends with him. He loved you guys a lot." And it was true.

"Oh honey, don't you worry. We're good. Just because two people aren't good together, doesn't mean they aren't good people."

She was right. I'd been married to a good man. He didn't cheat on me, or on our taxes. He worked hard, was a good father, and a good friend and neighbor. It was comforting to remember that.

"What are you looking for?" She asked.

I truly had no idea. Maybe something with a self-cooking kitchen and a large shoe closet??

For the last 25 years, we'd lived in 3 places-We started in an apartment after we married. We bought our first house before Aaron was born and upsized when the kids got bigger. These were "our" homes-a reflection of all of us and how we "lived". We had things like a recliner in the living room for Dad, and a separate game room for the kids. My ex-husband and I shared an en-suite bath and a walk-in closet. We kept a guest room for when we had family visiting. Two car garage. The usual stuff.

I had no idea how I "lived" yet. My life before was centered around my ex and the kids. I didn't know what my center was at the moment.

"Ummm. A house?" I said. With slightly more confidence I shared the price range in my budget.

"Great! I think we can find something for you. Do you know what kind you want? House, condo, townhome?" She asked.

"Not really."

"How many bedrooms?"

"Three? Maybe 2. Or 4."

"OK. Tell me about what you do, where you commute to work, where you like to go to have fun or shop."

I mostly worked from home and only went to the office once or twice a week. It was easy to get to from most places I might live. Fun?? I am newly divorced. I didn't have fun. Was I supposed to have fun? I assumed I was in some mourning period for divorcees. I had not even contemplated "fun." I shopped—because that's what I did—but lately, not even a killer pair of shoes could compete with the weight of a crumbling life. Maybe I should tell her I need to be close to a really good bakery and ice cream shop. Honestly, baked goods and ice cream seemed like more realistic needs for a mourning middle-aged divorcee.

"I think that I want to stay in this area close to my sister." I said. I was used to it here. There was an Amazon distribution center nearby, so I often got the same-day delivery option. I liked the nail salon I found. My sister and I had gotten into the habit of going to the Mexican place up from the high school for margaritas on Wednesday while my nephew was at basketball practice-they were $2 off and delicious.

"We will find you something, sweetie. Let's get together Saturday and I'll show you some. I got you," She said. "And Renee, call me anytime if you just want to talk, OK?"

"I will, Sharon."

Sharon and I did go look at some houses Saturday. We stopped at the Mexican place and had lunch and margaritas. And we talked. Sharon was always a good listener. And having gone through loss herself, she was very understanding. It's amazing how much healing can happen when you have someone to talk with who understands your pain, especially someone like Sharon. I felt a little lighter when I left, even though I had eaten my weight in chips and salsa.

We went to look again on Sunday after church, and found the perfect house. 3 bedrooms, 2 baths, a nice kitchen with a counter bar, living, dining, and 2 car garage. No shoe closet, but I would make do. But the really cool part was the backyard. It was like a park. The prior owners had landscaped all around the perimeter, and had added a beautiful covered outdoor living space and a fire pit. I could just imagine family barbecues in my backyard, dining al-fresco, cool nights by the fire pit. I was excited.

Wait! I was "excited"! I hadn't felt excited since, I couldn't remember when. Maybe it was January when Macy's had that after Christmas sale and I got those cute suede booties for half off? Perhaps. But this felt different. This felt good. I had something to look forward to. A future with barbecues and bonfires in it.

◆ ◆ ◆

We would close on the house in about 30 days, so I went about the next phase-furniture. When we divided the household goods, I got the guest room, my office and the kitchen table. I needed living and bedroom furniture including a bed.

I made my way to what had to be the world's largest home furniture store. It was two stories of retail ambition masquerading as a warehouse, stuffed to the ceiling with furniture, electronics, appliances, and an impressive selection of throw pillows. One-stop shopping, with twenty-four months, no interest financing. I wish they would make me that deal on shoes-there was a pair of Christian Louboutines I would like to have.

I settled on a creamy sectional with a matching ottoman, a blue club chair, and a brass-and-glass end table. A strange mix of softness and structure—cozy textures for comfort, metal and glass for light. I added a heap of throw pillows in assorted colors. So many that, realistically, only one or two people could sit on the sofa at a time. Which felt about right.

It was just me, after all.

I draped a taupe chenille blanket across the back of the chair —not folded neatly, but tossed, casual. Lived-in. I placed a tray on the ottoman with a small floral arrangement and a scented candle. Everything was soft, light, and warm.

And maybe, just maybe, it was also a tiny middle finger salute to my ex.

He hated throw pillows. Used to complain every time we visited my mother—said her living room felt like being tossed into a foam ball pit at Chuck E. Cheese. Maybe he would've hated this, too.

I moved on to the master bedroom—correction: my bedroom. That little pronoun change still felt wild.

I chose a simple set: bed, dresser, two nightstands. The saleswoman called it "transitional style," which I assumed meant "still figuring it out," so that was perfect. I had no idea what it actually meant, but I found the clean lines and warm wood tones simple and appealing.

I also picked out a stuffed chair and ottoman for a reading corner. I had gotten really good at reading in the living room while the family watched TV. Moms can read through anything—arguments, cartoons, Armageddon. It's one of our superpowers. But a quiet spot to read in a room all my own?

That felt like luxury.

As much as furnishing a post-divorce home for one could be considered a *luxury*. It felt a little sad if I thought about it.

I was headed down the tracks on the train to Pity Town again. It happened. I would be moving ahead, making a life for myself, and I would have these moments of sadness. Brief as they were, there was still such lingering sadness for what was, and now wasn't anymore.

I sat with the salesperson to finalize everything. She typed in my selections with the glee of someone about to hit her monthly sales bonus—and maybe name her baby after me. Then she looked up and asked, "What size bed do you want?" It felt like a pop quiz. Was she looking at me funny? Was her left eyebrow always raised like that?

"King." I said weakly. We always had a king-sized bed when we were married. When the kids were little and prone to crawling into bed with us in the middle of the night, we often pondered a *double* king-sized bed. But I am single now. The kids are gone. What does a king-sized bed say about me? Does a single woman with a king-sized bed say "Room for two here! Wink. Wink". "Single and ready to mingle!" Is that why she's giving me the side-eye-like I need remedial classes on morality and mattress selection?

Oh Lord. Is a single woman owning a king-sized bed a sign of an "easy woman?" And how and when might someone even see my king-sized bed of iniquity? My Mom would see it. Oh man! My Mom is going to think I'm a "woman of the night" (My Mom is too old fashioned to call me a slut.)

My thoughts continued to spiral, taking me to heights of anxiety I never before experienced when shopping for a bed. Does a king-sized bed lead to dating? Men? S-E-X? I am not ready for that. I told anyone who would listen that I was never dating or getting married ever again. I was still firmly planted in that field, thank you very much.

I knew what I had to do.

I bought a queen.

Crisis averted.

◆ ◆ ◆

The inspiration for my bedroom decor came from the most delicious duvet cover I'd ever seen—floral, soft, and warm. I added more pillows and a rose-colored Afghan. The result was a cozy little sanctuary. Comfortable, inviting… and absolutely not sexy. Nope, no one could possibly get the wrong idea.

And I had baskets.
Everywhere.
Trash baskets. Toilet paper baskets. Dryer sheet baskets.

Baskets for fake flowers, real flowers, and houseplants. If it could fit in a basket, it went in a basket.

The real splurge—the guiltiest of pleasures—was the coffee machine.
Caffeine and cute shoes had been my steady companions through the whole ordeal. I couldn't count on my marriage, my emotions, or my cell service, but I could count on coffee, and a sling back with a kitten heel.

I bought one of those sleek single-cup machines with the little pods, plus a cute basket to hold them.

This may have been a very intentional double middle finger salute to my ex.

When I was married, he insisted on brewing coffee in a pot. So, I let him have custody of Mister Coffee. I didn't even fight him for it.

And then I got myself a new machine.

One button. One cup. Just for me.

Divorce didn't have many perks, but it did come with French Roast on demand.

On some level, decorating my new home felt a little like an act of defiance. But compromise—that was marriage, wasn't it? You give up small things because the relationship matters more than throw pillows or coffee makers. And those were small things. Reasonable, even. I'm sure he made plenty of compromises for me, too.

The first night that I slept in my new house was bittersweet. The house had no memories of my kids or my past married life. It was a clean canvas. I felt a lot like that canvas-empty. I had hope, but I wasn't sure I had the palette of colors I needed to fill the canvas. Not yet anyway. Unlike when I moved in with my sister,

I was facing the finality of the end of my marriage completely alone.

I had to face facts.

My marriage was over.
This was my home now.
This was my bed now…wait, MY bed.

When you are married each spouse gets a "side." Rarely does that "side" change. My ex always wanted the side closest to the door. It occurred to me-I don't have a side in this bed. Sure, I'd gotten in bed on the side farthest from the door. But I didn't have to. I had both sides of this bed! This was *the queen's* bed. I could get in and out of my bed from any side. AND I could sleep on any side after I got in-even from the opposite side. I could get in on the left and sleep on the right. Or I could sleep in the middle! Wait, there's more.

My ex didn't like the top sheet tucked in at the bottom. He said it put too much pressure on his feet-as if that's a real thing. So, I never tucked the top sheet in. It made making the bed the next day like starting over. I could tuck in the top sheet now. With this new knowledge, I jumped out of bed, walked to the bottom and tucked in the top sheet with hospital corners. Then I walked around to MY other side of the bed and got in. I situated myself in the dead center of the bed, and used both pillows. With a grin of smug satisfaction, I feel asleep.

In the middle of the night, I untucked the top sheet-too much pressure on my feet.

As the days went on, I got into a rhythm.
I went to work. I went grocery shopping, I got my nails done, I did laundry.
Pretty soon when I laid my head on the pillow at night, in the center of the bed, flat sheet untucked, I found myself feeling more at home.

CHAPTER 3

When the kids left for college, we had gotten into the routine of doing a weekly FaceTime call together. It helped all three of us maintain some connection as they were moving off and moving on with their lives. I wasn't a fan of FaceTime. The camera angle made me look older and more washed out. I preferred Zoom-it had soft-focus. Every Monday night at 8, the three of us connected. Fortunately, we continued those calls even after the separation. I knew the kids were dealing with a lot of feelings about the divorce. I tried not to burden them with my own. Sometimes these calls would be short, their anger or frustration obvious. I felt if I could show them I was OK, they would be OK too. So, every Monday, I put on my best OK face and we had our calls.

We were on a Monday call a couple of weeks after I moved into my new home, when Aaron asked "So, how are you doing Mom?" This was what I called a landmine question. If you answered wrong, the whole conversation could blow up. And since the separation, he'd never asked this before. I took it as a good sign that he was asking now. Perhaps he has come to some terms with the divorce.

"I'm good," I said, and was a little surprised that this time, I meant it.

Morgan, the younger of the two and the more tender-hearted (that's a kinder way of saying dramatic) asked "Do you ever get lonely?"

"Not really," I said.

The truth was, sometimes I felt lonelier when I was married—

even when the house was full.

That kind of loneliness was sharp and noisy.

The loneliness I feel now is different.

Quieter.

It wasn't the sting of being ignored while folding someone else's laundry.
It wasn't refilling the snack drawer with his favorites, and never hearing *thank you.*

Maybe loneliness is not even the right word for what I feel now.

I wasn't lonely for people. I was *longing* for... something.

Purpose? Fulfillment?

A hobby that didn't involve loading the dishwasher or carpooling?

I didn't know yet. But at least now, no one was asking what's for dinner while I tried to figure it out.

"You should get a dog!" Morgan was an animal lover. As soon as she got out of college, she got a dog, a job and a roommate-in that order. I found her enthusiasm for pet ownership a little odd since we never had animals when she was growing up. Her Dad was allergic.

"No, thank you. I don't need a dog to clean up after. Uh uh, no." I protested.

"You might really like having a dog, mom, for company." Aaron added. Isn't it funny how kids think you get so lonely without them. I did miss them sometimes. But I think the teenage years prepare parents for their kids moving out. That's when they start ignoring you unless they want or need something-like food or clean clothes.

"Look for one about one to two years old, and female. Don't get a male. They mark everything." I had no idea why Aaron knew so much about dogs. He didn't have one that I knew of. Maybe his new girlfriend had one.

I was the last person who needed a dog. Dogs were a lot of work. I raised kids. I think dogs are harder. Kids grow up, they learn to make their own cereal, and sometimes, under threat of grounding or no cell phone, will clean up after themselves. Dogs require walking, feeding, and training. And until said training actually kicks in, there are even more messes to clean up.

On top of that, I had a sum total of zero experience with owning a pet of any kind. My parents got this idea that we needed a dog once. I was about 10 years old when my mom came home with a puppy-a Great Dane puppy. She was already raising six of us in a 1700 square foot 3 bed, two bath house. Maybe she thought she needed a 7th? I have no idea. She let my youngest brother name the dog. He named the dog…*Puppy*.

We had Puppy for about a week. And as I mentioned, until training kicks in, there are a lot of messes to clean. Us kids took turns cleaning the messes. I was grateful there were so many of us to take a turn. I wasn't often grateful to have so many siblings, nor to share a room with my three sisters. There was at least one benefit of having a dog, I guess.

One afternoon, Father Bartonelli, or Father B as he liked us to call him, had stopped by to visit my parents. We all loved Father B's visits. He always brought us kids lollipops. We were all sitting in the living room, and Puppy was seated majestically beside my mom. Without warning, the most horrific smell came wafting from the direction of my mom and the dog. My Mom noticed first, but was doing her level best to hide her reaction. Then it hit my father. His eyes started watering. Once us kids started to smell it, the mayhem rivaled a runaway train.

My youngest sister pinched her nose. "Ewww! Who tooted? Gross!" She whined. This started the rest of us kids waving our hands, pinching our noses and laughing. Even with Father B in the house, farts were funny to kids 10 and under. My Dad may have been trying not to laugh, too.

My mom dismissed us to our rooms, and we all quickly

complied. "Renee, please take Puppy outside?" Dad opened the back door. He was opening a window when I took the gassy dog, and put him in the backyard. But not before I noticed Father B grab a tissue and dab at his eyes.

The next day, Puppy was gone. My parents explained to us that there was just not enough room for Puppy to run around in our yard, so they took him to a farm to live.

We never had another pet.

"No dogs." I said, "End of discussion"

The following Saturday, I was at Home Depot for paint samples —soft yellow, maybe. I saw a sign for the pet store next door advertising a pet adoption, and my curiosity got the best of me. I was just going to look. Absolutely not getting a dog. Just a little window shopping for fur.

The adoption event was being held in a large room in the store used for classes. The event was well attended. There was a row of crates two high down the length of the room. If the rescue got a dollar for every "aww", they would have been self-funded. I wondered how many people were just looking, like me? For the dogs' sake, I hoped some would find their fur-ever home today. Tables lined the walls, and volunteers in matching t-shirts for the rescue organization stood about the room. I was greeted by a woman as I walked in.

"Welcome" she said. "Just let us know if you have any questions, or if you would like to spend some time with one of the pups. We have a visiting area so you can get to know each other."

"I'm just looking." I said, hoping that was a thing. Do people window shop for dogs? Heck, I tried on shoes that I never buy, so I was going for it.

I looked up and right in front of me in the top crate was the most adorable dog I had ever seen. It was a small dog, about the size of a chihuahua. It was tan colored, short haired, and had the most beautiful brown puppy dog eyes. Awww!

The dog watched me, and the volunteer followed close behind as I approached the crate. It never barked. It didn't move. It just watched me intently as I approached. There was an information sheet attached to the crate.

"Princess Sparkle Puppy" I said out loud. That was the name on the sheet.

"I let my daughter name the rescues. She's four," the volunteer said sheepishly over my shoulder.

"How sweet." I said.

I read further, and noticed that "Princess Sparkle Puppy" was in fact a boy. I said nothing. Frankly, I thought he could pull it off.

As it turned out "PSP" was about 6 months old and a chihuahua mix. He wasn't expected to get much bigger. Maybe twelve pounds. He'd been found abandoned on the side of the road. Aaron had told me to get a female and a little older, so he was out.

"Sorry little guy." And I walked away.

I continued down the line of crates. There were so many older dogs that had been surrendered or found abandoned. I wished someone with a farm would take them all home. They all deserved a better life, like Puppy.

I approached the last crate in the row. It held a mid-sized dog. Not too big, not too small. It had a beautiful coat of longer hair. I didn't know enough about dogs to be able to identify the breed. The dog backed up in the crate as I approached. "She's shy" I thought. I picked up the information sheet. It was a female, and her name was Elsa, no doubt another of the four-year-old's doing. She was presumed to be between one and two years old and fully grown. Some type of spaniel. Was this fate? Was I supposed to take Elsa home with me? Aaron said to get a female, 1-2 years old. I knelt in front of the crate and reached my hand out, just knowing that this was our moment when we would both feel our bond and know she was meant to come home with me.

My heart was racing with anticipation. Was this it? Was I about to find my dog soulmate? My companion for life-well, her life.

"Hi sweet girl." I cooed. That's when all Hell broke loose. Elsa lunged for me, barking wildly. I jumped back, knocking down one volunteer and one would-be adopter in the process.

"Oh shit,"

Her barking set off a cacophony of barking from the other dogs, and my expletive set off gasps from the other people. I was certain both could be heard in Home Depot.

What did she communicate to her dog friends that they were all barking? I felt like they were all yelling at me. Did they somehow know I wasn't a dog person? I wondered what I had done to offend her.

A little boy leaned over where I was sprawled on the floor.

"That's a bad word."

"It is. You should never say it."

"You owe me a quarter." He said, extending his little hand.

I got to my feet, and handed the boy his quarter.

I was heading for the door, still rattled and half-certain I'd been hexed by a room full of rescue dogs, when I looked back.

Princess Sparkle Puppy was sitting exactly where I'd left him—silent, still, and staring at me like he'd been expecting me all along.

No barking. No jumping. Just… waiting.

I had felt something when I first saw him, hadn't I? But I let the information sheet talk me out of it. A boy dog. Too young. Not the "right" fit on paper.

I'd done that before. Dismissed something good because it didn't check all the boxes.

I was going to try something different this time-I was going to go with what *felt* right.

I stopped walking. I stepped closer. He still didn't move—just held my gaze like he was giving me a second chance to get it right.

"Would you like to visit him," a volunteer asked.

"Yes, I would, please." I said.

"Come this way and I'll bring him to you." He led me to an area that was behind a privacy curtain. There was a chair, and some dog toys. Foam blocks were placed behind the curtain to keep the dog from leaving the area. I sat in the chair while he went and retrieved the dog. He returned, and sat him on the ground in front of me.

"He's still pretty small. You might want to sit on the ground with him," said the volunteer. "I'll be back to check on you in a bit."

After what happened with Elsa, I was hesitant. I slowly lowered myself to the floor, and the dog jumped in my lap and laid his head on my leg.

My heart melted like a popsicle in July. I was in love.

A few minutes later the volunteer peered in the curtain, "How's it going in here?"

I looked up at him from my seat on the floor, softly petting the sleeping dog in my lap. I didn't say a word.

"I'll just go get the paperwork started," he said. And off he went.

It didn't take long to complete the process of adoption. They handed me the dog- *my* dog-on a nylon leash, and we were free to go.

Fortunately, we were in a pet supply store, so I grabbed a cart, and Princess Sparkle Puppy and I were off. I was greeted by a store attendant. He was tall and gangly. He could have been 16 or 21.

"That's a cute little guy. What's his name?" He asked.

I was impressed that he knew it was a male without checking under the hood.

"His name is...'Prince," I didn't want to start my day as a dog mom by embarrassing him with the name "Princess Sparkle Puppy", so I decided on the fly to shorten it to Prince.

"I just got him. And I need everything."

"No problem." He said. "Let's start simple, a collar. This way." He took me to an aisle where we selected a collar and a leash. The attendant, Eric, suggested a harness that deters pulling when you are walking the dog. I guess I will be walking the dog. That sounded nice.

Next, Eric took me over to crates. "You plan to crate-train?" He asked.

Eric must have sensed from my hesitation and deer in the headlights facial contortion that I had no idea what he was talking about. He simply grabbed a crate and cushion and threw it in the cart.

We made a full circuit of the store, with Eric guiding me to the things I needed-food, dishes, training treats. Eric had suggested I do a new pet owner training. It was once a week for six weeks, and I would learn how to be a good pet owner. The classes were held in the store, in the same room where the adoption event took place. I signed up.

Eric loaded up my car for me. Too bad he couldn't follow me home to get the 40lb bag of dog food out of the car too. He helped me install the seat cover in the back seat (He installed it while I snuggled Prince.) Then he showed me how to secure Prince for car rides.

Two clicks later, I headed home with a backseat full of kibble and commitment.

I was a dog mom.

CHAPTER 4

Life with Prince turned out to be everything and nothing like I expected. It was certainly a lot of work, but the love and companionship I felt with him made it worthwhile.

Once we got home, I set up Prince's crate, got his food and water prepared for him, set out some piddle pads and sat on the floor. Prince waddled over, squatted, and peed—three inches from the piddle pad. I guess aiming is optional when you're cute.

"Ugh"

Then he walked over to where I was sitting, climbed into my lap, licked my hand and fell asleep.

"Awww."

◆ ◆ ◆

By the time Prince and I were scheduled to go to our first training class, I was feeling like a new parent again-sleep deprived. Prince didn't sleep through the night. He would wake up and whine, at which point, I would carry him outside to take care of his business, then with a kiss on his little head, place him back in his crate. He woke much earlier than I would normally wake up, but not so early that I could go back to sleep.

On the day of our first class, I finished work early and grabbed dinner consisting of a bowl of cereal. I ate cereal for dinner now. It was fast and easy. I had not yet figured out how to cook a meal for one, nor did I feel inclined to make the effort. I put on a pair of shorts and a t-shirt. I wasn't sure what we would be doing in this class, so I went casual and wore my tennis shoes. Side note —why do we call all athletic shoes "tennis shoes" in the South?

I've never picked up a racket in my life. And I'm pretty sure mine were technically "running shoes"—not that they've ever seen me run. Unless you count shoe sales. But I got a really good deal on these at *Off the Rack,* and they were cute.

I arrived at the store a little early, and walked into the room where training was held carrying my little student in my arms-his first day of school. I captured the moment with a photo on my phone. Prince was gaining quite a followership on Instagram. The room was arranged now with about eight chairs all in a circle with a large space in the middle. I was first to arrive, so I took a seat, and placed Prince on the floor beside me.

Minutes later people started arriving. A younger couple walked in with a bigger hairy dog, a German Shepherd maybe. The dog didn't make a sound as it entered. The couple sat, and the dog dutifully sat beside them. I was immediately concerned. Was I in the right class? Their dog was sitting quietly. Prince was moving around the room as far as the leash would allow him. He was jumping and playing with what could have only been some imaginary friend-lost in a world of his own making.

Before my mind had the time to work up some good angst over the situation, a young woman walked in, being pulled by a dog almost as big as she was. It could have been a Great Dane. It kind of looked like what I remembered of Puppy. Upon seeing the other dogs, her dog began to bark loudly and run at the German Shepherd. The German Shepherd never moved as the other dog jumped on him (or her, I didn't have a chance to lift its leg and look). Prince cowered behind my leg. I placed a hand down just in case the big dog lunged for Prince. I suspected Prince would have been a tasty snack for a dog that size. A middle-aged man walked in with a Blue Heeler-I knew a Blue Heeler because one of my boyfriends in high school had one. Her name was Betty. She was crazy! And so was this one. She saw the Great Dane and joined in the fun. The two dogs were wrestling in the center of the chair circle, their owners trying to wrangle them by pulling on the leashes. It was total insanity.

A man walked in alone, holding something black that looked like a key fob. He pressed the button, and the dogs instantly went silent. Each ran to their owner — the Great Dane pacing in front of the little woman, the blue heeler cowering behind his — a man sweating and breathing hard from the strain. If he went down, I was covered — I'd taken CPR at the Y.

"Hey y'all. I'm Liam. I will be your instructor for this class. If everyone would please take a seat, we can get started." Liam lowered himself into a chair with no trouble from his dog, but the little woman was pulling on the leash and getting nowhere. The couple with the well-behaved German shepherd just sat there with smug expressions. I was starting to think their dog wasn't real. Probably some high-end robotic model — no shedding, no barking, no soul.

Liam approached the little woman and her dog, and in a gruff voice said "Sit." The little woman startled at his tone, and abruptly sat in a chair. And I'll be damned if the dog didn't sit too. I was in awe. Whatever that super power was, I wanted it. Liam now had my full attention.

Once everyone was settled, we went around the room and made introductions.

The couple with the German Shepherd were Jerome and Lisa. The dog was Daisy. They were experienced dog people. Obvy. Little woman was Priya, and her dog, which was a Great Dane, was Karma. Like me, Priya was new to dog parenting. Also, obvy. The man was Jorge. His dog's name was Elbow. He let his 5-year-old nephew name him—which explained everything.

We concluded the first class, and I was inspired. Liam had an easy way about him, and he made dog training and ownership seem easy and practical. I went home armed with some new techniques, and homework. Prince and I would be perfecting "sit" to proudly demonstrate in the next class.

Liam approached me after class. "He is really adorable. Where did you get him?" He crouched down but Prince growled, like a warning for Liam to step back. That was a first. Maybe he does not like men.

"I got him here. At an adoption event, last weekend actually."

"Be sure to get him checked by your vet as soon as possible." he said warily. I had not considered that. The rescue volunteer said that they had him checked by a vet, had all of his shots, and had been neutered. They had given me some paperwork to that effect.

"Thanks. I will."

"I use the vet clinic in Northlake. I like them and they have late and weekend office hours."

"I will give them a try then. Thanks." I started to walk away.

He touched my shoulder and handed me a business card. "Here. If you have any questions, feel free to text or call."

I took it, nodding like the responsible pet owner I was. This felt very official. Like I was being entrusted with a direct line to tech support for my dog.

"Thanks," I said, and smiled.

He smiled back.

I assumed he gave these to everyone.

I took Prince home, and tossed the card onto the kitchen counter with the junk mail and a flyer for gutter cleaning. It was a dog training card. Nothing more. Right?

On Friday night, my sister, Amy, came over. We were going to order pizza and rent a movie. My nephew was at a sleepover.

Amy picked up Liam's card from the kitchen counter.

"That's the dog trainer. I am taking Prince to dog training." I explained.

"OK, but why do you have his card?"

"He gave it to me."

"He gave it to you."

"Yes." I was confused. I had a dog trainer. He gave me his card in case I had questions. About dog training. What was the mystery?

"I thought you were going to training at the pet supply store?" she asked.

"I am. Why?"

"Is this a private training?"

"No. Amy, what?" I was tired of the cagey questions. What was she getting to?

"So how old is this trainer?"

"40's, maybe? I don't know Amy, why?" I replied, my exasperation evident.

"I think he likes you." She said, grinning.

"Why would you think that?" I thought that was preposterous. Laughable. I laughed, "HA! No way."

"They usually have different trainers rotate through the class. Did he give everyone his card?"

"Probably" I said, but I wasn't sure. Did he? "I wasn't paying that much attention at that point." Come to think of it, I didn't see him approach anyone else after class.

"See, he likes you. What will you do if he asks you out."

Amy was enjoying this way too much. I, on the other hand, was frozen in terror. It had been too long since I dated. I had met my ex right out of college. We dated two years before we married. I was better prepared to conduct brain surgery than I was to go on a date.

So, yeah — Amy had to be wrong. Liam wasn't into me; he was just a helpful dog trainer. I grabbed the popcorn and fled to the living room.

"Bring the wine, would ya?"

◆ ◆ ◆

As Liam suggested, I scheduled an appointment for Prince with the vet. Prince and I arrived at the vet's office, but not before Prince dropped a special package in my back seat. Fortunately, I had a washable cover in the backseat, and poop bags. Poop bags are the glamorous side of pet ownership—tiny shopping bags you use to pick up steaming deposits and protect other dogs from their baffling instinct to eat each other's poop.

I walked into the lobby with Prince on a leash and a warm pile of regret in a plastic bag-tied shut but still mocking me.

The receptionist looked up and smiled. "I'll take that." she said. More gladly than she should have been, she relieved me of my bag of poop, ducked in the back and returned empty handed. "We will be able to check for heart worms with that." Prince must have known. Such a smart boy. "This must be Prince."

"This is Prince." I beamed proudly.

She came around the desk and took the leash from me. She walked him over to a large scale, and Prince jumped up to stand on it.

"8 pounds, 8 ounces." She led him off the scale and over to the desk where she wrote his weight on a form. "I will take him back and be back to get you started on some paperwork." She picked him up and ducked into the back. She returned a bit later and gave me a stack of papers to complete.

I returned the completed paperwork, and she ushered me into a small room with another door at the back. The room held only a chair and a small exam table. "The Doctor will be in shortly."

I wasn't waiting long, when the other door in the room opened, and Liam walked in carrying Prince. He was dressed in blue scrubs. His name badge said "Bill".

Bill, huh? Odd. But maybe this was his 'professional vet tech' name.

"I thought I recognized this dog." He said. "How is Prince doing?" His tone was all business; unlike the more casual tone he used in the pet training. His voice sounded deeper. Maybe it was the close quarters.

"Doing great!" I said. "Are you a vet too?"

I was more than a little uncomfortable now after what Amy said. Or maybe it was his cologne—he smelled amazing. Clean and woodsy, like he owned matching towels and flossed regularly. I wasn't sure the last time I'd even noticed something like that.

I reminded myself that Amy was wrong. This wasn't flirting. And there wasn't anything wrong with appreciating good grooming… as a concept.

"No Ma'am. I am Dr. Robertson's vet tech. He's checking some of Prince's test results and will be right in," he replied.

He no sooner said the words when the vet walked in. He was a middle-aged man, and at least a foot taller than me. "Hi I am Dr. Robertson."

Liam ducked out quietly, with a nod.

Dr. Robertson went about his exam.

It turned out that Prince was in exceptional health for a puppy who was likely about 8 weeks old-not six months old. Dr. Robertson explained that he could tell by the dog's teeth. He also let me know that Prince would likely grow to about thirty pounds. It was all good news to me. I didn't care how much he weighed. He was my boy.

I never got a chance to ask Liam about the name tag before Prince and I left the vet office.

Like Amy said, the training class did have a few different instructors. Liam wasn't there for every class. But all of the instructors were good. The six weeks flew by, and Prince and I were both learning. We had mastered sit, shake and high five. He was too impatient to manage "stay" for longer than a count of thirty, and too curious to "leave it." But we knew what to work on going forward. The most important accomplishment was that Prince had become potty trained. It was much easier than I anticipated. I was proud of us both.

It was the last class, which included a quick review of the skills we learned, an overview of the advanced training class offered (for the bargain price of $399), and a little celebration with cookies and dog biscuits. Liam was our instructor. I got an adorable picture of Prince wearing a little mortar board cap for Instagram.

Class was over, and I was about to leave, when Liam approached.

"Hey, got a minute?" he asked.

"Sure," I said. "What's up?" I was much more relaxed around Liam, now that six weeks had gone by and he'd not once asked me out. Amy was clearly wrong. I will never let her live that down.

"I was wondering if you might want to meet me for a drink sometime?" He asked.

"Uh" I stammered. The blood drained from my face; air froze in my lungs. My vision went blurry. Was I having a stroke?

"I wanted to wait 'til after class was over. I hope you don't think this is weird." He said.

"No, not weird." I said. It was totally weird. Not that he asked, but that he asked *me*. I assumed I was wearing a sign that said "No Dating Allowed". I know I had one when I was married. I guess it was the ring. They should make single, not ready to mingle rings, so you know when someone is in the do-not-ask-me-out zone.

And damn it-Amy was right. I will never live that down.

I looked at Liam. He was funny. Kind. Cute in a clean-shaven, owns-more-than-one-shirt kind of way. He was the right age, had a steady job, and didn't say anything weird about his mother.

Eight months post-separation, this was the kind of man I should say yes to.

Objectively, he was a logical choice.

I wasn't twenty anymore—I wasn't looking for fireworks. I was looking for decent. Safe. Low risk of future therapy bills.

He ticked every box:

— Male

— Gainfully employed

— No facial tattoos

— Expressed interest

According to every article, podcast, and well-meaning friend, I was supposed to be ready by now.

"Sure. That sounds nice." I said. And was shocked that I did.

"Great" He seemed relieved. "What's your number, I'll call you? I am working this weekend, but how would next week work for you?"

"Next week is good." I gave Liam my phone number.

"See you next week." He said, and beamed a smile at me.

"See you next week", I smiled back, and left.

I walked Prince to the car, wondering what in the hell I had just agreed to.

I got to the car, and immediately called my sister. "You were right. And I think I'm going on a date."

Liam called me Monday evening while he was on duty at the fire station. We made plans to meet up for a drink on Wednesday. I hoped Amy wouldn't be disappointed to miss out on margarita night.

We talked on the phone for almost two hours, before he was called away. I learned he was an only child, raised in central Texas. He'd been divorced for a few years, but had no children of his own. He called his ex-wife crazy. That's all he said. I told myself not to read too much into it. It made me wonder if my ex called me crazy. I cringed at the thought.

I asked Liam about the name tag from the vet office. He explained that his given name was William, but that his Mom always called him Liam. When he was in middle school, he changed it to Bill. He answers to either, but preferred that I called him Liam.

Still, the conversation with Liam was easy, and I found myself enjoying it and looking forward to our date. I may have even been smiling when we hung up.

Liam and I had agreed to meet for a drink at 6 at a little wine place with a full bar and tapas-style plates. Amy assured me it was a good first date spot. First dates, she said, should be short —just coffee or a drink. No dinner, no movie. Just enough to see if more time might be worth it. I made a mental note for future reference.

Amy came by at 4:30 to help me decide what to wear. She

brought a few of her own things for me to try on. It was August, which meant HOT in Texas. It also meant you could expect frigid indoor temps courtesy of overzealous air conditioning. What I immediately learned was that my wardrobe was as unprepared for dating as I was. My wardrobe included clothes for conference calls (yoga pants and a nice shirt), clothes for shopping (yoga pants and a nice shirt), clothes for when I went into the office (jeans and a nice shirt, or sometimes slacks and a sweater), and a few outfits for when I traveled (including yoga pants for the flight). I had a collection of hoodies to rival the entirety of my nephew's basketball team. What could I say-I liked a good hoodie, and they looked so cute with yoga pants. I went with a sundress of my sisters, paired with a platform-heeled strappy sandal from my shoe collection. I styled my hair, did my make up. I was as ready as I was going to be.

I walked out to the living room where Amy was busy texting on her phone. She looked up, and smiled.

"You look great!" she beamed. "Are you ready?"

"I guess so," I said. I was only ready on the outside. On the inside, I wasn't ready for this in the slightest. This felt like a really bad idea-like "trying a new hair cut a week before the wedding" bad idea.

"I have something for you." She rummaged through her purse and pulled out a box and handed it to me. It was a box of condoms.

I almost dropped the box like it was anthrax.

"Wh-what are these for?" I asked.

"Come on Renee. You cannot tell me you don't know what those are for." she replied.

"Not what I meant." I said tersely. "I mean, why do I need these?-DON"T ANSWER THAT," I stopped her before she could say more. I got the feeling she was really enjoying this.

"Renee, safety is important. It's not just about kids, there are all kinds of diseases," she said matter of factly.

"You told me that a first date was short, and just to see if another date was worthwhile. I don't think we need condoms for that."

"If you are lucky, you might."

I rolled my eyes and walked the box of condoms to my room. I threw them on my dresser. But they felt a little too conspicuous there. So, I picked them up and threw them into the drawer in my night stand. But what if I forgot about them, and one of the kids went in my room and found them? I went to my sock drawer and grabbed a sock. I wrapped the box in the sock, buried it in the bottom of the drawer, and layered other socks on top. I stashed it like I used to stash Target receipts when we were "on a budget." But safer. And with better cotton blends.

Satisfied that I had successfully hidden the condoms from prying eyes, I grabbed my purse and was out the door.

I was going on a date.

CHAPTER 5

It was 102 degrees, and after circling for parking, I settled for a spot a quarter mile away. I walked as slowly as possible, but nerves and heat combined had me sweating like I'd sprinted. By the time I reached for the door, sweat was running down my face and pooling between my boobs. I couldn't have felt any less attractive. The scorching door handle almost convinced me to turn around and go home.

I was immediately relieved when I walked in and felt the cold blast of air conditioning in the vestibule. I sighed like someone emerging from a desert—and not just because Texas in August was trying to kill me. I approached the hostess and asked for a table for two. With a smile, she parted a heavy curtain and revealed the dining room—equal parts romance novel and speakeasy.

The room beyond was dimly lit and trying very hard to be mysterious. A polished wood bar stretched along the left wall, complete with a brass footrail and the kind of lighting that made everyone look ten percent hotter.

Across the room, a giant fireplace tried very hard to make "cozy" happen in August. Flanking it were two emerald velvet sofas-because nothing says "drink responsibly" like letting people lounge on luxury upholstery. Scattered small tables flickered with candlelight made it feel like I was meeting to trade state secrets, or just be overcharged for artisan olives.

Overall, the atmosphere was warm and casual. I tried to mirror it, aiming for a look that said effortless and charming instead of mildly panicked. My nerves, however, were staging a coup. I took a deep breath and gave myself a silent pep talk: *it's just a drink with your dog-trainer/vet tech. You're a grown-ass woman. You've survived labor, divorce, and group texts with the PTA. You have insurance and matching Tupperware lids. You can do this.*

The hostess seated me at a table for two, and promptly brought me a glass of ice water-instantly earning my affections. I excused myself and went to the bathroom to clean up. As I looked in the mirror and worked on the damage, I wondered what I was doing here. I didn't feel ready for dating. I wasn't sure that I even wanted to date, much less forge a relationship with someone ever. Maybe it was just too soon. Maybe anytime would feel too soon. This was a bad idea. I had decided I was going to wait for Liam, and then just be honest with him, and explain that I wasn't ready. I hoped he would understand.

With a solid plan in place, the flood of anxiety receded. I walked out of the bathroom and returned to the table with purpose. And there was Liam, seated at the table. I was reconsidering a run for it, but he looked up, smiled and as I approached the table, he stood.

"Hi," I said.

He looked really good. Unfairly good. The kind of good that made my brain forget words for a second. He wore a gray t-shirt that somehow managed to look both casual and curated—like it had been made just for him—and jeans that didn't try too hard, but definitely succeeded. And boots. Of course he wore boots. He was raised in Central Texas. Boots were practically a birthright.

"Hi," he replied, then leaned in and kissed my cheek. He smelled amazing again—clean, warm, a little woodsy. The kind of scent that made you want to lean in and stay there a moment too long.

My resolve gave a suspicious creak.

Then he walked around and pulled out my chair. Like, actually pulled it out and waited. I couldn't remember the last time someone did that.

And just like that, I was in trouble.

I took my seat and when Liam sat in front of me, he gave me another of his killer megawatt smiles. Was it hot in here? I ignored any inclination to guzzle the ice water, taking dainty sips while we made small talk. I had not worked up the courage yet to tell him I was leaving.

The waiter appeared. "Hi. My name is Matt. I will be taking care of you today. What can I get started for you?"

Liam gestured to me to go first. OK, one drink, then I am out of here.

"I'd like a glass of chardonnay, please."

"Yes ma'am. Would you like the 6oz or 9oz pour?"

"6 please." The smaller the pour, the faster I could get out of here.

"And you sir?"

Liam replied in a silly English accent, "William does so love a good chardonnay on a warm afternoon. I'll have the same. 9 ounces for me, good man."

The waiter just chuckled and said "Coming right up, sire." He smiled at me and walked away.

Okay. That was cute, if not a little odd.

We settled into comfortable conversation by the time the waiter brought the wine. In fact, it was so easy and comfortable that I didn't think to leave. I was enjoying myself. Liam was really good at telling stories. He would use different voices, and was very animated at times. His three different professions gave him plenty of material for a good story. It was another glass of wine and almost 9 by the time we walked outside, where it was still 95 degrees-but much more tolerable.

Liam walked me to my car. When we got there, I noticed something odd. My car was running. Fantastic.

"This is your car?" Liam asked, almost laughing.

"Yes. I must have forgotten to turn it off when I jumped out." Nerves, I guess. I was really embarrassed. Time for a quick and graceful exit.

"It's late. I'm gonna go. Thanks for tonight." I said as I turned toward the driver's door.

He reached out for my arm. "Can I see you again?"

Any embarrassment I was feeling gave way to total surprise. This man-smart, funny, and polite-showed up for drinks with me-a sweaty, anxious, awkward mess; a woman so ditzy that she left her car running-and wanted to see me again.

"Yes. I'd like that."

"Great. Well, good night, Renee."

Liam leaned in.

I stiffened. He wasn't going to kiss me, was he? Amy didn't say anything about first-date kissing. She did buy me condoms, so... if *that* was on the table, then surely kissing made the cut.

Now, if I could just remember how.

It had been months since I kissed anyone—and that was marriage kissing: a quick drive-by for hello, goodbye, or good night. Lips barely involved. Passion was usually reserved for Tuesdays, Thursdays, and the occasional Saturday... also known as "grown-up time."

Was I supposed to tilt my head? Which way? What do I do with my hands? Was there a refresher course? A manual?

He got closer... and kissed me.

On the cheek.

Well, *that* was disappointing. I'd prepped like I was about to parallel park in front of a patio full of brunch people—only to notice the valet sign.

Liam was walking away, when he turned back to me. "Please text me so I know you made it home ok."

"OK." I said.

He started to walk away again, but turned one more time "I might smile all the way home."

He was smiling. And so was I.

I smiled all the way home. I had a nice evening with an attractive, interesting man, who wanted to see me again. That felt good. More importantly, I survived my first date.

Once I got home, I let Prince out of his crate. I snuggled him as I carried him into the hall, and got him outfitted with his harness and leash ready for a walk. We got back and I realized I had not yet texted Liam. It was after 10, but I dropped him a quick text anyway.

Me: Hey. I'm home. Safe and sound. Thank you again. I had a great time.

Liam: Kinda late for a text, don't you think?

Me: I'm sorry. I took Prince out when I got home.

Liam: It's OK. Next time. We don't want Billy to worry about his best gal.

Me: OK. Sorry again. Good night.

Something was starting to niggle at me — not quite a red flag, but definitely a yellow one. I told myself it was just a text. Just a joke. Just me overthinking, again.

But who was *Billy*?

I didn't hear from Liam at all on Thursday.

Maybe texting him so late was a deal killer.

He had said something about "next time," but now I wasn't so sure.

I debated texting him again to apologize—then realized what a small relief it was to not hear from him.

Maybe I just wasn't that invested.

So, I left it alone.

Liam texted me on Friday. I was in the office holding a staff meeting when my phone buzzed.

Liam: Hi beautiful.

Then he sent a smiley face emoji.

Then he sent a gif of a cartoon dog holding a bouquet of flowers.

Then he sent a smiley emoji.

Then he sent a sad face emoji.

My team noticed the buzzing coming from my phone. I casually sat on it, as if that would make it less obvious.

The steady stream of texts felt... excessive.

But maybe he just had more free time than a nine-to-fiver like me.

He was a firefighter. Lots of downtime between emergencies, right?

I told myself not to read too much into it.

Still—

This was the same guy who got irritated when I called ten minutes late.

And now he's questioning my boundaries?

Once the meeting was over, I replied.

Me: Sorry, I was in a staff meeting. Hi!

Liam: Took you long enough.

Ok, I was getting irritated. I had a rule with my kids that they could only blow me up at work if someone was bleeding, and I had better be the second call after 9-1-1. When I was at work, they understood that I owed the company my time and attention. I couldn't imagine how Liam didn't understand that.

Me: Staff meeting.

Liam: Right. Go see a movie with me tonight?

I wasn't sure that I wanted to do that. Things were starting to feel like more than I was up for.

Me: I'm not sure I can. I'll get back with you later. I have someone in my office.

Liam: I just really want to see you again.

Ugh.

I *really* wanted to say no.

But then I wondered—was I just looking for reasons to say no? Was this self-sabotage?

Me: OK. Come by at 6 and we will see what's playing. OK?

Liam: Yeah!!!

He included a confetti gif.

Then a smiley face.

I turned off my phone until I left the office.

◆ ◆ ◆

As I drove home from work, I realized I wasn't looking forward to my date. It all just felt like too much. Maybe I wasn't ready to date yet. I wished I wanted to—really wanted to—but I couldn't summon the energy to care. I figured I'd tell Liam after the movie. At least we were going to a movie, which meant limited talking and even less emotional heavy lifting.

I didn't bother changing out of my work clothes. Still in jeans and a nice-enough shirt, I opened the door to find him standing there, hands in his pockets, head down like a teenager about to confess something.

"Hey! Come on in."

He glanced up briefly and walked past me, kissing my cheek on the way. The spark was gone—replaced by something quiet and broody, which only made the knot in my stomach pull tighter.

"Beer? Soft drink?" I offered, trying to reset the tone.

"Beer would be great, thanks," he said, and dropped onto my couch like he owned a spot there.

I grabbed one from the fridge and handed it to him, then sat beside him with my phone to look for movies. He leaned back, crossed his ankle over his knee, and surveyed my living room like he was checking for resale value. No interest in the movie options. Just silence and a beer.

"Nice place," he said finally.

"Thanks."

"You sure have a lot of throw pillows." He added, lobbing two onto the chair like they had personally offended him.

His tone was strange. Slower. Heavily accented—more than usual. Was this a Texas thing or a new character he was trying out? It didn't feel like a joke. It didn't feel like Liam. I grabbed my phone and pulled up local movies.

"What about this one? It's a comedy," I offered, reading the title and cast.

"Nah. Don't like that guy. Why? Is that a movie you'd pick?"

His voice had taken on a drawl that sounded suspiciously like a bad Matthew McConaughey impression—but off, like he was trying to sound casual and landed somewhere near creepy.

"We can pick something else. What kind of movies do you like?"

"I'd like for you to answer the question," he said flatly.

Okay. "I probably would see it, sure. But it's not a big deal. We'll find something else."

He shook his head slightly. "Figures. Anyone dumb enough to leave their car running would probably like that movie. Ha." He took another sip.

I blinked. Did he just insult me? In my own house? With my beer?

I stood slowly. "You know, Liam, I think this isn't such a great idea. I think you should go."

That's when everything shifted. His body language changed in an instant—gone was the smug recline. Now he looked up at me, small, almost folded in on himself. His voice softened to something uncertain and strange.

"Don't be mad. I'm sorry. Please? I'll watch whatever you want."

The voice was childlike. Pleading. The drawl was gone. The sudden shift was jarring. Uncomfortable had become deeply unsettling.

I kept my phone in my hand. Just in case. My heart was racing but I forced my legs to carry me to the door.

I opened it. "Good night, Liam."

He stood, drained the rest of his beer, and tossed the empty can onto the coffee table. A deliberate move. It landed with a thud that sounded bigger than it should have.

Then he walked out.

But just before the door closed behind him, he turned, looked me up and down with disdain, and—back in the McConaughey voice —said "Call me when you change your mind."

I slammed the door. Locked it. Deadbolted it. All in one breath.

Then I let myself slide to the floor. Shaking. Furious with myself for letting him in at all.

Why did I even agree to go out with him in the first place? I knew I wasn't ready.

I don't think I will ever be ready for that!

Who would be?

I pulled up his number, and blocked it.

Goodbye, Liam.

Then I texted my sister.

"Code Pink."

CHAPTER 6

My sister Amy and I were what you called "Irish twins"-she was born nine and a half months after me. We had always been close. Neither of us settled far from where we grew up, while our other siblings were flung from coast to coast- a brother in Boston, a brother in Chicago, a sister in Long Beach, and my youngest sister in Houston. Even when I went off to college, Amy followed me to Lubbock.

We started "Code Pink" in college. "Code Pink" meant that one of us had a really bad date or a bad break up and needed the other to talk to, and some Pink Panty Droppers-a silly little college girl drink that Amy and I still favored in times of crisis like man troubles.

Amy rang the doorbell. "Why is the door locked? You never lock your door."

"You'll never believe me when I tell you" I was still shaking.

She walked in with a grocery bag. She set it on the kitchen counter, and gave me a hug.

"Where's the pitcher?" She asked.

"I don't have one." It felt like just one more kick in the pants. First Liam turns out to be a nut job, and I didn't even have a pitcher for Pink Panty Droppers. This is what my life had come to.

Choo-choo! The train to Pity Town is pulling in the station again. All aboard.

"No problem. I got this" Amy rummaged through my cabinets, and pulled out a large metal bowl. She dumped the two-liter

Fresca, the can of pink lemonade and the vodka into the bowl. I think I saw her add extra vodka. Best sister ever! She stirred it up, and tried pouring it into our glasses. She abandoned that quickly, and grabbed two aluminum straws instead. She handed one of the straws to me.

"Cheers," she said, and clinked her straw to mine.

I sat at the bar with my head over the bowl, straw in my hand, and told Amy what happened. I felt naive. No, stupid- I felt stupid. Embarrassed. Ashamed. How did I not see it? I knew how I didn't see it, I wasn't prepared for dating.

"I don't think I'll ever date again." I took a big gulp from the bowl.

"Sure you will, just not maybe right away." she said. "Don't write anything off yet. You never know. Keep an open mind."

I didn't feel like having an open mind. I felt inadequate—like a broken IKEA shelf: wobbly, misaligned, and held together by sheer will and duct tape.

Honestly, I'd felt that way since before the separation. I couldn't keep my marriage together, and now I couldn't even make solid dating choices. I took another big sip and gave myself brain-freeze. Perfect. Even my coping mechanisms were poorly executed.

"Amy, this was just such an epic fail on top of all my other epic fails." I said wincing.

"Stop. You are not allowed to do that. You didn't fail. You tried. Sometimes things don't work out. So, what? You get up and try again. You will learn from this, and be better next time." This was our mantra- we don't fail, we learn.

"No next time. I'm done." And took another drink, a smaller one this time. I was starting to feel a little more relaxed, either from the unburdening, the drinking, or both.

"Ok. For now. Maybe you need a little more time. Maybe try going on a lot of first dates and see what you like."

"Mmmm" I liked the "More time" part of her plan, not on board with the rest.

"In the meanwhile, your toys will get a workout." And she laughed.

I had no idea what she was referring to. I looked at her questioningly.

"Oh, come on Renee, you can't tell me you don't have any toys?"

"I got rid of all the kid's toys when they outgrew them. I do have dog toys." I said.

"Tomorrow, we are going to the toy store. Every single girl, Hell, every girl-needs toys."

Oh no. *Toys.* That's what she meant??

I awoke the next day, slightly hung over, but feeling generally better. I just wanted to forget that I ever went out with Liam (and all of his personalities), and get back to normal-whatever *that* was.

Amy showed up with a to-go coffee and a breakfast biscuit. She knew me so well. I popped a couple of Ibuprofen, crated Prince with a kiss on the head, and followed her out the door.

We were about halfway to the store, still in disbelief that we were going shopping for a... I had no idea what the appropriate term was. *Dildo?* That was a legit word in the *New York Times* Spelling Bee, so maybe it was fine. Or was it a *vibrator*? That one passed the NYT test, too. Was there a difference? Was I supposed to know the difference?

I was afraid of what ads might start showing up in my Pinterest feed if I googled "difference between vibrator and dildo."

Then it hit me — I hadn't even considered what I was wearing.

Was there a dress code for sex toy shopping? Should I have gone for that "20-something on a bachelorette trip" vibe — stilettos, mini skirt, and a sash that says something my mother would blush at?

I glanced at Amy. She was in denim shorts, a sleeveless top, and flip-flops—basically my exact outfit. Okay, at least I wouldn't be underdressed for... this.

The whole thing felt scandalous. I wasn't sure if that was exciting or horrifying.

Maybe both.

Amy pulled in, and parked facing the main street through the middle of town. "They don't have parking around the back? What if someone sees us parked here?"

The shopping center housed exactly four shops. The sex toy store just happened to be wedged between a CBD shop and a foot massage place — both with reputations that made the sex toy store look classy. The only other place was a Wing Stop — because after a good foot massage, who doesn't crave wings and a CBD chaser?

"If anyone sees us, just tell them we were here for wings." I said.

Amy rolled her eyes. "Let's go." She reached for her door.

"Wait! What's our backstory? Where are the hats and wigs so we can disguise ourselves?"

Amy was out of patience with me.

I swear some days I think we were raised by different people. "Renee! Stop! We are not robbing a bank. We are two grown-ass women going to a store to buy a dildo. There is nothing wrong with that. Now get your ass out of this car now!"

I was almost positive our catholic grandmother might disagree. But I was committed to being more open-minded and trying new things. I got out of the car, and despite the Texas heat, I sprinted for the door- sweaty boobs be damned. I quickly opened the door to 'Satin Sin' and rushed inside. I bent over to catch my breath, and Amy strolled in behind me, shaking her head.

From the outside, the store windows showed tasteful images—couples holding hands in parks, smiling at sunsets.

Inside, it took a tawdry turn: giant posters of men and women mid-ecstasy, faces frozen in orgasmic bliss.

I suddenly wondered what my face looked like "in the moment"—poster-worthy, or like I'd just stepped on a Lego?

Once I got past the artwork, I noticed that the store was one big room. There was shelving on the left of bottles of lubricant and massage oils. There was an array of scents and flavors, and even had gluten-free, sugar free, and vegan options for those on restricted diets.

To the right were racks of lingerie- think if Victoria Secret had a super slutty sister lingerie. More lace and strings than fabric. I couldn't tell if some pieces were meant for the top or the bottom...or both. Amy walked over to a rack and grabbed what I think was a pink teddy. She pulled it off the hanger and threw it on the floor.

"Amy! What are you doing?" I whispered loudly.

"I am seeing what it looks like in a heap on the floor. Once a guy sees me in this, that's where it would end up."

I am not sure what "guy" Amy is referring to. She doesn't talk about her boyfriends. In the ten years since her husband died, I have never met one.

I picked up the teddy and put it back on the hanger. I wondered if *I* had a slutty sister, and if I envied her.

A girl approached us. "Welcome in. I'm Tiffany, and I will be your Pleasure Consultant today. Have you shopped with us before?"

"Yes."
"No."

Tiffany was young, and I mean *really* young. I think I had socks older than Tiffany. I wondered just how much experience she had to be qualified as a "Pleasure Consultant." Not that I had a strong opinion about an appropriate age for a Pleasure Consultant given this was my first encounter with one. Considering the options, I was glad she was a woman. I couldn't imagine having a man. And I guessed being young was ok-preferential to someone my Mom's age. It made me think of that gynecologist I saw once who looked like my Dad's twin brother. That was uncomfortable.

"What can I help you with?" She asked.

Amy looked at me expectantly.

"I...am...ah...looking for a...um..." All I could do was gesture to the wall of mechanized dicks.

"She is shopping for a vibrator." Amy blurted. "Good grief."

"Nice." said Tiffany. "Do you own any toys already?"

"Oh no..." Once I read a particularly racy book, where a couple used a toy together. I asked my ex if that was something he would be interested in. He let me know he would be all the toys I needed. I never mentioned it again.

"Do you know if you prefer vaginal or clitoral stimulation?" I had to hand it to Tiffany, she was handling this with clinical efficiency.

I was staring at Tiffany now like she was speaking a foreign language.

"Let's start simple then." She grabbed one of the brightly colored devices from the shelf. This is a good model for a beginner such as yourself. It's very popular. And good for either-very versatile. It is also soft and gentle. Here, feel for yourself."

She handed me the device, and I was surprised by how little it looked like its biological counterpart. I would call it more ergonomic than anatomically representative. I wasn't sure what

I was supposed to be "feeling" for. It didn't feel real- neither the vibrator in my hand, nor the fact that I had a dildo in my hand *in public*. It was hot pink-I liked the color.

Tiffany gestured to another model. That one definitely looked like the real thing, except for the color- lime green. She then launched into a TED Talk about clitoral vs. vaginal stimulation, with diagrams, features, and app integrations. I barely registered a word past 'remote control.'

"I have that one. It's ah-mazing!!" Amy chimed in.

I felt completely out of my element, and like less of a woman for it. This pre-teen knew more about sexual gratification than I did. It was embarrassing.

"I'm just going to look around."

Tiffany smiled. "Of course, just let me know if you have any questions."

Amy and I walked in silence.

"How is it you and I were raised by the same parents, and you know this stuff and I don't." I asked her.

"I didn't learn it from Mom if that's what you're asking. I don't remember, really. I think it was friends. But it's OK, Renee. If it's not for you, it's OK. But I just thought it might be something you would enjoy. "

Could I try? The truth was, I wished I could be more like Amy. She was such a free spirit. She cared so little for what others thought of her. To be honest, I was a little curious.

I threw caution to the wind, and chose the hot pink model.

I met Tiffany at the register.

"Excellent choice." She was pleased, and I felt oddly validated, like I'd aced the final in a *Dildo 101* class. "Do you need any lubricant or toy cleaner? 20% off with purchase."

"I'm good, thanks."

"If you have any questions, you can always come back here, or you can scan the QR code on the box. It launches their video library. The instructional videos can be very helpful." I had no words. Videos?

Tiffany gave me the total. "Satin Sin supports the Town Senior Center. Would you like to add a donation to your total today? It is tax deductible. We are giving away a bottle of strawberry massage oil with any donation of $5 or more."

"That's so nice," Amy said.

"We are their largest donor." Tiffany beamed proudly.

"I thought North Way Boots was their biggest donor"

"That's us!" she exclaimed. "We go by 'North Way Boots'- you'll see that on your credit card statement. Discretion and all."

I understood completely.

We completed the transaction and walked out. Discretion apparently didn't extend to their shopping bags-this one was bright yellow with "Satin Sin" in bold black letters legible from space. I hid the bag as best I could as I sprinted for the car. Amy took her sweet time walking to the car to unlock it, leaving me facing the main road with a bag of dildo in my hand.

"That strawberry massage oil is mine. Payment for bringing you." She let me know as she started the car.

As we drove away, I realized—I was OK.

It wasn't about the dildo. It was about not apologizing for wanting something.

The simple act of buying a sex toy had made me feel more empowered than I ever had before.

I was a woman who owned a dildo.

I just hoped my mother never found out.

DEBORAH KEDZIERSKI

I was proud of myself.

CHAPTER 7

It was Labor Day, and Amy's neighborhood club was hosting its annual end-of-summer pool party. In Texas, this holiday signals the start of pumpkin spice season and 50% off Christmas décor —never mind that it's still 102 degrees, and we'll be sweating well into October.

I made a batch of chocolate chip cookies to bring. Then I donned my tankini and a pair of shorts-my version of socially acceptable swimwear. I grabbed a hat, towel, and SPF 100 sunscreen, then headed out.

We met at Amy's and the three of us made our way to the clubhouse. We arrived early enough that Amy and I got lounge chairs. Mattie saw some friends and was off. The association had given us each two drink tickets, and were serving a variety of weak frozen cocktails. I got a strawberry daiquiri and Amy grabbed a margarita.

Drink in hand, we made our way back to our chairs. I proceeded to slather on the sunscreen, donned my floppy hat and sat to take in all of the merriment around me, and perhaps a nap.

Amy was very outgoing, so it was no surprise when she kept jumping up to greet people as they arrived. I found myself feeling a little envious—she made friends so easily. I still had a few close friends, but things felt...off. Normally, holidays like this meant hosting or attending some kind of gathering, but this year, Amy's was the only invitation I got. Since the divorce, loyalties seemed to have quietly shifted. Maybe people were just uncomfortable with divorce. Maybe they thought it was contagious—like one hangout with me and their marriage would implode by morning.

I wondered if my ex was at those get-togethers, or if he, too, had to find something else to do.

"Thanks for inviting me." I said to Amy when she'd returned.

"Of course."

"You're lucky to have so many friends"

"Friends and sisters. Cheers!"

We clinked solo cups- no glass allowed by the pool.

"You have friends. They will come back around. They just need some time," she said. It occurred to me- a marriage is not just two people. It includes kids, in-laws, nieces and nephews, and friends. The impact of a divorce is far reaching. Everyone needs time to adjust.

"Maybe you need to make new friends," she suggested. "Maybe join a gym, or a club of some kind."

Sitting there in a swimsuit, half-marinated in SPF 100 and self-consciousness, I decided joining a gym sounded like a responsible life choice. I had no idea which gym, or what I'd actually do there—maybe stand near the weights and pretend to stretch.

Then I remembered that guy at the courthouse mentioning a run club. Maybe I'd check it out.

I could get in better shape, meet people, and maybe Prince would enjoy running with me.

Sure, I'd never run more than a mile in my life- in middle school- but how hard could it be?

I had shoes. I had a dog. I had vague enthusiasm.

What could possibly go wrong?

◆ ◆ ◆

Two days later, I wrapped up work a little early. I put on a pair of shorts and a t-shirt with my running shoes- fortunately I had running shoes though only because they were cute. I pulled my hair back into a ponytail, and put Prince in his crate with a treat and a kiss on his sweet little head. Then I headed out.

Moonwinks was a bar in an old building off the square in Denton. The space was long and narrow with high ceilings and a staircase off to the right. There was a sign for Denton Run/Walk, with an arrow pointing toward the stairs. I climbed to the third floor which led to a covered roof top bar area. The place was empty except for one woman seated at a longer table.

"Hi," I said.

The woman looked like she'd stepped out of a fitness catalog—sleek running gear, shiny black hair in a perfect pony tail, and not a drop of sweat in sight. She was wearing running shorts with a matching top and the trim on her white running shoes matched the color of her shorts. I, on the other hand, looked like a refugee from a garage sale-wearing my son's old gym shorts, a ratty t-shirt, and a ball cap I got at the last staff retreat.

"Hi. Are you here for the run club?" She had a perfect smile, and was wearing just enough make-up to enhance her natural beauty. I looked like someone who wandered in by mistake.

"I am," I replied.

"Welcome! I'm Disha."

"Renee."

"Nice to meet you. A little about us, we run-or walk-a three-mile loop" She showed me the loop on a map. "We usually leave here right at 6. Then we meet back up here for a drink. The bar gives us happy hour pricing on drinks and apps 'til 7:30."

"Sounds great." I wondered if I should just leave at 6 and head to my car.

"Are you a runner?" she asked

"No." I said.

"That's ok. We have lots of walkers, too. Just go at your own pace." That made me feel a little better. I walked Prince every night. Maybe I could start with the walkers.

I sat down across from her, and while we waited for others, Disha and I chatted and got to know each other. She was about 10 years younger than me, never married. She worked in a marketing firm. She was a runner, and started this group about four years ago. She helped me get connected with the group on Facebook and Instagram. I genuinely liked her.

People started trickling in. A few minutes before 6, I spotted the guy I'd met at the courthouse.

What a relief—he wasn't a murderer.

Embezzler? Still possible. That would take more time to suss out.

He moved through the group with ease, handing out smiles, back pats, and hugs like a politician on primary day.

Clearly, he had friends here.

Then he made his way over to me.

"You made it!" he exclaimed. "Remember me? From the court house?"

"I do, yes. But I apologize, I forgot your name."

"David."

"Renee." We shook hands.

David was smiling at me. Easy, warm. The kind of smile that made it impossible not to return it.

"So, you *are* a runner."

"Actually, no."

"Well, you will be soon." He winked. "Have you met Disha?"

"I did."

"She's great. Let me introduce you around."

We started walking and meeting some of the other members, and I was surprised—pleasantly.

I'd expected a sea of sleek, spandex-clad gazelles.

Instead, there were all kinds of people: young, old, tall, short, chiseled, squishy, and everything in between.

Basically, it looked like a group of humans, instead of the Justice League.

I exhaled. Maybe I wouldn't have to fake a sprained ankle after all.

At 6, we all started heading down the stairs, and people took off walking and running. David was still right beside me. Disha joined us.

"Ready?" She asked.

"Renee is not a runner yet, so let's pace with her." David suggested.

"Works for me." Disha said.

"See that tree next to the book shop on the right? Let's run there. Then we'll walk a bit. Go slow and easy." David suggested.

We took off. David continued to pick landmarks along the route —a bookstore here, a bench there. I gasped through each one, lungs on fire, thighs staging a full rebellion. It was excruciating. But they never left my side. They each offered encouragement and advice along the way.

By the time Moonwinks came into view, I felt like I'd climbed Everest.

"Woo! You did it, Renee!" Disha celebrated. "You *are* a runner now." David said.

Was I? I always thought a runner was someone who ran well. Disha and David acted like being a runner was as simple as trying. I did try, and I finished. That felt good.

It was still in the 90's outside, so I soaked through every thread of my clothes. My face was the color of a tomato. I'd thrown my hat off at the one-mile mark, and my ponytail was mostly fallen, hair matted to my face and neck. Neither David nor Disha were breathing heavily, and Disha looked as fresh as a daisy. The cool air at Moonwinks felt like a well-earned reward. David and Disha kept going, and I just stared at the stairs. My legs felt like Jello- if Jello caused excruciating pain- I wasn't sure they would make the climb back up. How bad would it be to take the elevator? I told myself that there was ice water up there, and maybe a cold beer and some cheese fries, so up I went.

People were milling around, drinks in hand. There were cups and pitchers of ice water on the tables. It would have been impolite to throw ice water on myself, so I settled for chugging a glass. I then ordered myself a beer- who knew beer would taste so good! After a hot run, it really hit the spot. Disha and David were sitting at a table and motioned for me to join them. There were two other guys there, and another girl about Disha's age. I remembered David introducing them to me- Pete, Sam, and Carrie.

"Cheers to Renee's first run today." David hoisted his glass. "Well done."

The rest of us followed suit. "Thanks!"

"You might be sore tomorrow." Disha offered. "You might want to stretch when you get home. I usually do some yoga stretches. Helps with soreness."

"You like yoga?" I asked. "I have never been but wondered about it."

"I love it." She gushed. "It is so relaxing but you also get such a great workout. On Saturday mornings, Yummy Yoga offers free classes. They do it so the new yoga instructors can practice. Wanna go?"

"Sure!" I said. We exchanged numbers, and made plans to meet for yoga on Saturday morning.

I finished my beer and got up to leave. "Thank you, Disha, David, for running with me. I'm sorry that I slowed you guys down. But I really appreciate the help."

"No problem"

"Happy to."

"Nice to meet you all. Good night."

"See you next week?" David asked.

"Yup, See you next week."

It felt like more than just finishing a three-mile loop.

I'd tried something new—sweaty, messy, and wildly outside my comfort zone.

And I hadn't died.

I felt proud. Not the kind you post on social media, but the kind you tuck in your back pocket and carry around quietly—like a little secret between you and your sore thighs.

More than that, I felt welcome. Like maybe I belonged here.

These people didn't know anything about my past.

They didn't care.

They liked me sweaty and out of breath and slightly delirious—and I liked them, too.

I wanted to come back.

I wanted to see where this could go.

DEBORAH KEDZIERSKI

I was a runner.

CHAPTER 8

The next morning, I was questioning my life choices. Who takes up running on purpose at my age? My legs hurt in places I thought were purely decorative. I shuffled around the block with Prince, groaned my way into a chair, and discovered that even using the bathroom had become an exercise in humiliation.

Maybe for lunch, I would look up a stretching video on YouTube.

I felt better by the third day, and tried running in the mornings before work. I did a lot more walking- slowly- the first few days until the soreness abated. It turned out to be a great start to my day. I noticed it got a little easier with each run.

That Saturday, I met Disha for yoga—and surprise of all surprises: I loved it. Somehow, it was both relaxing and invigorating, like a spa day that also toned your arms. Disha swore it would make me a better runner, and honestly, if she'd said it would make taxes easier, I'd have believed her. At this point, I'd try anything to make running feel less like slow-motion dying.

After class, we grabbed coffee.

Disha was a remarkable person. I learned that she worked five jobs while she was in college. She was from a large family, and had to do whatever she could to help out her parents financially. She was a tri-athlete working towards an Ironman. She was also generous with her time and talents. She served on the board for a children's charity, and helped plan their fundraisers. She was easy to talk to-very genuine. And most importantly, she loved shoes almost as much as me. She was someone I would be glad to call my friend.

After coffee, she took me to a store that specialized in running shoes. Apparently running shoes were not just a fashion statement. Who knew? We were greeted by a cheerful, athletic, young woman.

"Welcome in. How can I help you?" She asked sweetly.

We let her know I was a new runner in need of shoes.

"Have you been fit for shoes before?" She asked.

"No."

"No problem. Follow me over here, and we'll get started." She took us to an area where they had two treadmills. She guided me to one of the treadmills, and had me run.

With head snapping quickness, that sweet girl morphed into an evil drill sergeant before my eyes. She paced around the treadmill, barking at me to change everything—my posture, my stride, the way my foot was striking.

Oh, my foot wanted to strike all right—it wanted to strike her right in the butt. She even remarked that I wasn't breathing properly. I was breathing *wrong*? Was that even possible? I mean- in, out, in, out. Wasn't that right? I was still conscious, after all.

After a few minutes, she let me know I could stop. I was grateful, and a little sweaty. And just like that, she was back to being the sweet girl we met when we came in- she got me a nice cool glass of water and offered me a seat while she got some shoes to try on.

Thirty minutes later, we left with new running shoes in hand. We also had a new run club member. The sales person, Ashley, didn't have anywhere to run on Wednesdays, and Disha just happened to have a flyer with her. Ever the marketeer, she also convinced the store manager to let her leave run club flyers at the register for other customers, and to meet with her later in the week about sponsoring a run. She was incredible.

Disha left, and I made my way over to the sporting goods store.

I left with a shopping bag full of color-coordinated running apparel.

I was ready to run.

◆ ◆ ◆

The following Wednesday, dressed head to toe in my new running gear, I showed up for run club with most of the gang from the week before, including David. He saw me and walked over.

"We didn't scare you off, I see."

"Not a chance." I smiled.

Before we headed downstairs, I saw Ashley walk in and waved her over. I couldn't help but notice how her appearance turned a few heads, while she seemed completely oblivious. I introduced her to David. He introduced her to the others. Remembering I was new to running, she offered to run with me, and give me some pointers. I agreed—for the first mile. Then I planned to cut her loose to chase the wind at her own speed. I couldn't help but notice how she was eyeing Scott when he walked in. Scott was about her age, a marathon runner, and really cute.

At 6, we all made our way outside. Disha and David stood beside me.

"Slow and steady?" David asked.

"You guys go ahead. Ashley offered to run with me today. Have fun."

"You sure? We don't mind."

"I'm sure. But thanks! "

David and Disha took off. Ashley came out then.

"Ready?"

And we took off.

◆ ◆ ◆

Ashley was going to kill me. She pushed me hard. I went much faster and farther than the week before. But she also shared techniques with me along the way. I was grateful for her help, even if it would lead me to an early grave. I also learned a little about Ashley. Fitness was her vocation and her passion. She proved to be an exceptional instructor, pushing just enough to challenge me, but not to actually do any permanent damage.

We hit the first mile mark, and I encouraged her to go on ahead. I slowed my pace slightly and, keeping in mind the new things Ashley taught me, I went about the remainder of the course, alternately running and walking- but at no point, dying.

I was a little over two miles in when I spotted David running toward me from the opposite direction.
Did I take a wrong turn? Totally possible in my exercise-induced stupor.
He caught up, turned around, and matched my pace.

"What are you doing?" I barely got the words out.

"I saw Ashley was back, so I turned around. Didn't think you should be running by yourself. Safety in numbers."

"Thanks. Worried I might keel over?" I asked, laughing.

"Ashley blew by me at warp speed. If you were going to die, it would've been in the first mile."

We ran side by side, David easily keeping pace with my snail-like shuffle.

"When I saw you at the courthouse, you'd just come from mediation? Is that over?"

"Yeah. It is." His voice carried both relief and resignation.

"Do you mind me asking what happened? You don't have to tell me."

"I don't mind. She was unhappy... then met someone at work who made her happy." He gave a half-shrug that didn't quite hide the hurt.

"I'm really sorry."

"It's OK. I'm glad she's happy now. And so am I." He gave me a small smile, but I could still see the edges of the hurt.

"What about you?" he asked.

"Short answer — I was unhappy. Suggested counseling. My ex said it was *my* problem, so *I* should go. So I did. A few years later, I figured out my problem was... my ex. Specifically, his unwillingness to put in the work. I told him I'd keep trying, just not solo. He told me to file the papers. One thing I figured out in counseling — you have to own your own happiness. No one can give it to you."

"Hmmm. Own your own happiness. I like that. You're a wise woman, Renee."

"Call me Confucius — or maybe Yoda would be better. Short like me."

He smiled at me — easy, open, like we'd been friends forever and just didn't know it yet.

We kept talking, learning little bits about each other (as much as I could between gulps of air), and before I knew it, we were staring up at the godforsaken stairs to the third floor of Moonwinks. Whoever thought putting a bar for sweaty, exhausted runners at the top of Pike's Peak clearly hated humanity. David bounded up like it was nothing. I followed like someone who had just discovered her quads had a dark side.

At the top, we grabbed beers and joined the group at the table. Today, it was Disha, Ashley, Scott, Pete, and Lonnie. Lonnie was almost my father's age but in better shape than some of the guys my son's age. He, too, was a marathon runner.

"How did it go today?" Disha asked me.

"Better, I think." I didn't *look* better. By the end of the run, my shirt was half untucked, one shoe was a dull brown from a puddle incident, and my hair had escaped the ponytail like it was making a break for freedom. Any makeup I'd started with was long gone, replaced by the kind of sweaty glow you only see in workout commercials — except mine didn't look aspirational.

"She did great. No way my mom could've done that—uh, not that you're old or anything—sorry." Ashley caught herself. I resisted the urge to thank her for her service to the AARP. I looked over at David, who I'd guessed was close to my age. He sipped his beer and rolled his eyes.

"You know, Renee, there is a 5k coming up for Halloween. Some of us are going to run it. It's a lot of fun, you run in costumes, and they have refreshments, and a big dance at the end. Are you interested?" Disha asked.

Dumb question—how far is 5K? Hopefully not five miles. Please let it be closer to one. Why didn't I pay attention when we covered the metric system in fourth grade?

"How far is that?" I quickly scanned my friends for any eyerolls.

"It's only 3.1 miles," David replied. "Not much farther than you ran today." He made it sound like no big deal, like it was something I could do.

"It sounds like fun. Sure". It did.

Disha shared the details and I pulled out my phone and signed up.

"If you want, I can put this app on your phone that will help you work up to running a 5k. You just run 3 times a week, and you will be running a 5k in 6 weeks." David offered.

I unlocked my phone, and handed it to David. He did some things, and handed it back.

"I put my number in, just in case you want someone to run with."

"Thanks." I said.

"Take my number, too. I'll run with you anytime." Ashley said.

Before we left, everyone at the table had everyone else's numbers.

These weren't just strangers who ran past me anymore. They were names in my phone, people who believed I could run a 5K - and against all logic, I almost believed it too.

CHAPTER 9

In the weeks leading up to the Halloween 5K, I followed David's app like it held the secret to unlocking your potential in just three runs a week. I even mapped a neighborhood route that avoided hills, loose dogs, and overly creepy neighbors.

I kept going to Wednesday run club. Sometimes it got rained out. On those days, we'd text the group to see if anyone still wanted to meet up—maybe just for a drink. When we did run, I usually started out on my own, but by halfway through, David would show up and run with me. Each week, I ran a little more and walked a little less.

Race day arrived—Saturday night before Halloween. I knew David was going as a pirate and Disha was going as Peter Pan. I picked Tinkerbell. I wore my hair up in a bun and threw a leaf-green dress over my running shorts and sports bra. I pinned wings to the back and tied little pompoms to my shoes. A little glitter powder on my face, and I was ready. I thought the costume was clever—and still practical for running.

The race was at Texas Motor Speedway. There were cones marking the course and a stage set up near the finish line. I parked and went to check in. They gave me a number, which I pinned to my front. I took the T-shirt and race packet back to the car. I had a shirt from a run—the calling card of a true athlete. Or at least of someone who shows up and doesn't die. Good enough in my book.

I was nervous. Between the weather and my schedule, I hadn't made it all the way through the 5K app. I hadn't actually run the full 3 miles on any of the Wednesdays. Though I walked less than before, I still needed breaks. Maybe this was a terrible idea.

Could someone get disqualified from a 5K?

Was there a time limit?

Would someone ride up on a golf cart and politely ask me to stop embarrassing myself?

Would I be banned from run club?

Have to turn in my T-shirt?

Be blacklisted at the Nike store?

I considered faking a sudden case of food poisoning and going home. But I'd already pinned on the number. And the wings. And the pom-poms. I looked too cute to quit now.

I found the group. Pete, Scott, and Ashley were already there.

"Hey!"

"You look so cute!" Ashley said.

"Thanks. Look at you guys—wow!"

Pete was dressed as a clown, complete with seriously impressive makeup: white face, red mouth, blue and green stars around his eyes. He wore a curly red wig, a big red nose, and clown shoes over his running shoes. Ashley and Scott were in all black, wearing Ray-Bans—Trinity and Neo in running shoes. No one had said anything yet, but we were all pretty sure they were dating. The matching costumes, the lingering looks, the way they stretched in sync like a Nike ad—subtle as a confetti cannon.

Disha and David showed up next. Disha's hair was tucked under her hat. She wore green shorts and a matching Peter Pan shirt. She was adorable. David looked like Jack Sparrow from the waist up: flouncy white shirt, brown vest, belt, wig, fake beard, and black eye makeup. He was almost unrecognizable. I was impressed. These people took their fun seriously.

We agreed on a post-race meetup spot and headed to the starting line. Faster runners moved up front, slower ones further back, walkers behind them. I was relieved to see walkers. Any fears of being the slowest vanished. I lined up in the back of the slow runners, in front of the walkers—AKA the "slower than a turtle" section.

I assumed the rest of the group was up ahead, so I was surprised when David appeared beside me.

"What are you doing back here? Don't you need to move up a bit?" I teased.

"It's your first 5K. I'm going to run with you."

It threw me off. Why would he do that? I hated the idea that he was slowing down just for me. It was thoughtful. Sweet even. But I was used to doing things on my own.

Before I could protest, the race started. The crowd moved forward in a slow, collective shuffle—like we were all reluctantly boarding a rollercoaster we couldn't get off. But as soon as we crossed the starting line, the pack thinned out—fast runners darting to the left, walkers easing off to the right... and a handsome pirate jogging beside me like it was completely normal to run 3.1 miles in eyeliner and a puffy shirt.

"Slow and steady," David said, and we took off.

At a quarter mile, he asked, "You ready to walk?"

"Nope. I'm good." And I was. We kept going.

We chatted as we ran, and every half mile or so, he asked if I wanted to walk. So far, I didn't.

Then came the hill—going up, not down. I slowed to a crawl, and David started running circles around me like an overly enthusiastic golden retriever.

"We'll stop at the top," he offered.

"No," I grunted, unable to form full syllables but unwilling to give in.

At the top, my breathing evened out. Then, without warning, David veered off. "See you at the finish!" he called over his shoulder.

I rounded a corner about a quarter mile later. My legs ached, but I refused to stop.

Then I saw it—the finish line, just a hundred yards ahead. Goosebumps rose along my arms. My eyes filled with tears. I was overwhelmed by pride and fierce joy—the kind that shows up when determination wins and the voice in your head that said "you can't" finally shuts up.

I swear I could hear the theme song to *Rocky* in my head the closer I got to the finish.

As I got closer, I saw them—my running group, my friends— jumping, waving, cheering like they'd always believed I could do it, even when I hadn't.

David and Disha had their phones out, snapping pictures.

I crossed the line and stopped. I let it sink in.

I did it. I ran the whole 5K without stopping.

I didn't trip. I didn't die. No paramedics were involved.

Inside, I was crying, laughing, doing cartwheels.

Okay, maybe a little crying on the outside, too.

I did it—not for anyone else. Just for me.

I walked toward my friends—my very own cheer squad, minus the pom-poms. There were high fives, hugs, and the kind of laughter that makes your face hurt.

I felt like the star of a very sweaty feel-good movie.

It wasn't just about the run. I'd done something hard. I kept showing up.

And maybe—just maybe—I could start to believe in myself the way they already did.

***

Past the finish line, sponsors had tents set up with swag and refreshments. We grabbed bananas, bottles of water, and a protein bar that tasted like raisin-covered shoe leather and had the texture of a gritty fruit roll-up. Mine went straight to the trash.

I did score a nice ball cap from the local chiropractor's office to replace the one I ditched on my first run.

A local party band started playing once the last runner finished. No one was dancing yet, until David pulled me and Disha into the open space in front of the stage.

David, it turned out, could dance. Like...really dance. If Jack Sparrow had rhythm and core strength. We spent the next two hours laughing and spinning under the lights. Pete's clown moves were somewhere between interpretive dance and electrocution. We were gasping with laughter.

Eventually, the band finished and we made our way to the parking lot. Pete peeled off to his car. We walked to Disha's car first.

"Get ready for the Turkey Trot. Next month," Disha said.

Fantastic. My calves had just stopped hating me, and now we were penciling in their next protest.

"Okay! Good night."

David walked me to my car next.

"So, how's it feel? You ran your first 5k!"

"It feels incredible. But ask me again tomorrow when I am too sore to get out of bed." I replied.

" You'll be fine," He laughed. "We worked out all the soreness on the dance floor."

We got to my car. We stood there for the briefest minute. I wanted to hug him or something, but I did not want to be weird.

"See you Wednesday?" He broke the silence.

"I'll be there."

"Text me when you get home please, so I know you made it."

"Okay." That was sweet.

"And Renee, great job tonight. Really. "

"Thanks," it felt like high praise coming from David.

"Good night"

I texted David when I got home, as promised. Disha had already posted pictures from the race on the club page and mentioned me finishing my first 5K. Other members chimed in with congratulations. I felt humbled and grateful for the incredible support from these people—my friends.

What a night. I danced. I ran. I lived to tell the tale. And I got a T-shirt—which, let's be honest, is basically the adult version of a gold star. And I earned it.

CHAPTER 10

I had gotten into a new routine. I ran most mornings and walked Prince in the evenings. I worked. I met Amy for margaritas, but on Tuesdays instead of Wednesdays. I met Disha for yoga on Saturdays, church on Sundays. FaceTime with the kids on Mondays. I was getting comfortable.

Every week at run club, I would start running, and David would finish, and double back to run with me.

The first run club after the Halloween run, David doubled back as usual. We fell into our pace, chatting like we always did — swapping little bits about work, life, and whatever random thing popped into our heads. There was an ease to it, the kind of rhythm you don't have to work at.

Somewhere between me grumbling about the hills and him agreeing that the third-floor stairs to Moonwinks should be illegal, he asked, "So... have you started dating again?"

It wasn't nosy, just the kind of question friends ask when they've logged enough miles together to skip small talk.

"Went on one date," I said. "Realized I'm not ready. Might never be ready."

He nodded. "Fair enough."

"Honestly," I added, "I'd rather face these godforsaken hills than another awkward dinner with a stranger."

We finished the run side by side, no rush to fill the silence. Comfortable, like we'd been doing this forever — or at least long enough that he wasn't judging my gasping for air as performance art. It was... nice.

Thanksgiving was just 11 days away. I was on the Monday FaceTime call with Aaron and Morgan. Everyone seemed to be fine, but there was a tension for some reason. It was Morgan who finally broke it.

"Mom, we need to tell you something." This didn't sound good.

"Ok."

"I don't know what to do." She sounded so distraught. She could have broken a nail or found out her bestie had cancer. Her emotional spectrum was short, and heavy on the dramatic side.

"Stop being dramatic and just tell her already." Aaron said. He didn't have much patience with Morgan sometimes.

"Tell me what?" Now I was worried.

"Dad has a girlfriend."

I felt the blood rush from my face. I felt the world stop.

Just as quickly, I remembered I was on FaceTime, and I could not let the kids see anything on my face. They had struggled enough. Everything they thought they knew about their parents had been turned inside out. I felt like as the Mom, I had to help them navigate the murky waters of post-divorce parents. He could thank me later- as if.

I would find my own compass after the call.

"Ok." I said. "Is that it?" I went with the "act like you don't care" strategy. Of course, I did care, I just didn't have time to unpack why at the moment.

"No. Dad says we have to go with them to ski in New Mexico for Christmas. He is paying for us all to go." She whined. Morgan tended to do that.

I was becoming less ok with each new detail. If my face matched my feelings- my violent raging feelings- it might do more harm than good. They both knew all of my tells, so I had to deliver an Oscar-worthy performance.

"That sounds nice, Morgan. I'm not sure I understand what the problem is." I replied. I impressed myself. Thank you to members of the Academy for this prestigious award.

"Mom! You don't understand. We would be away for Christmas Eve AND Christmas Day. We won't be able to be with *you*."

I definitely got that.

I don't know where the inspiration came from for what I was about to say, but I knew this was some Mother-of-the-Year shit.

"First sweetheart, you are an adult. Neither your Father nor I can make you do anything. You are off the payroll so to speak. What you choose to do, on any day of your life, is your decision. You and Aaron may marry someday, and have kids of your own, and how you spend holidays will change- it should change. Change is constant.

"Second, it sounds like your dad just wants to have a nice Christmas with you and your brother. We can celebrate Christmas together when you get back. It's ok."

Morgan was quiet. I was patting myself on the back for taking the high road, when I really just wanted to tell them their father was the worst kind of poopy head.

"Aaron, ok?" He hadn't said anything.

"If you're ok, Mom. I don't want you to think we abandoned you on Christmas." He said.

"I'll be fine. Don't worry about me. And we will celebrate when you get back. We can still do all the things we normally do, or we can do some new things, just on a different day."

Boom! Mic drop. I should write a book about parenting. *Volume One: How to Lie Gracefully for the Sake of Your Children.*

Everyone seemed better when we ended the call. Aaron said very little, which means he had plenty to say, but wasn't ready. I would call and talk to him another time. Just the two of us.

I wasn't ok. Call ended, I let my face do whatever it wanted- go crazy. And it wanted blood.

I leashed Prince, and we went for a brisk walk. I thought a walk would help me process better, and release some of the pent-up energy.

Girlfriend? Seriously? We were pushing 50, in a couple of years. We were close anyway. Do 50-year-old men have girlfriends? It sounds childish. And how serious is this that he is introducing her to the kids? He never kept a car for more than two years. How long will *this* last?

It stung more than I wanted to admit. I imagined her—tall, smooth-skinned, stretch-mark-free, the kind of woman who looks amazing in a bikini and doesn't have to try. Everything I wasn't, or at least didn't feel like anymore.

Honestly, I had no idea what she saw in my middle-aged, paunchy, balding ex. It's not like he was rich. And he turned his nose up at coffee pods—because apparently, that's where he draws the line.

Prince's little legs were moving fast to keep up. I was deep in thought and forgot to stop to do his business.

Ski trip? Since when did he go skiing? We never did anything remotely physical on our vacations. If he wasn't in a lounge chair on a beach having drinks delivered, it wasn't a true vacation to him. We took the kids to Disney, and he booked a beach weekend for the two of us right after so he could "recover."

I noticed Prince was starting to lag behind me. I slowed a little.

But *Christmas*? Like he was St. Nick himself. Ha! He only participated in Christmas when cookies were involved- and just the eating parts. I did all the shopping, decorating, baking, wrapping, and cooking. He ate. That's it.

Prince abruptly stopped and sat down. I had worn him out. I picked him up and carried him.

The kids would be gone for Christmas. My parents were going to see my brother in Chicago this year. Amy and Mattie were going to Houston to be with my sister, Ellie. I would be alone- well, Prince and I would be alone.

I walked home and let him into the yard.

He sniffed a spot, turned twice, and pooped.

Yup. That just about sums it up.

The next night after I got home from margs with Amy, I called Aaron when I knew he would be home from work.

"Hey, Mom."

"Hey, kiddo. Just wanted to check in. How is everything going?"

"Good. Busy. Year-end sales push."

"You didn't say much last night." I was hoping it was the opener he needed to tell me what was bugging him.

"It's just really weird, Mom. I just want to stay out of it, but I feel like I am being dragged into some tug of war between you and Dad all the time." Weird was an understatement.

"I'm sorry sweetheart. I know this is hard. But for what it's worth, I don't want this to be any harder on you and Morgan than it already is. I don't mean to drag you into things. I am sorry if I've made you feel that way."

"I don't know that you have, but when Dad says he wants to take a trip for Christmas, I feel like he's asking me to choose one of you over the other. If I go, I hurt you. If I don't go, I hurt him."

"You are not going to hurt me by going skiing for Christmas.

It sounds like a lot of fun, and I want you to enjoy your holiday. I don't think your Dad is asking you to choose. I am sure it's as simple as he wants to do something fun with you guys for the holidays. Really, I'll miss you, but I'll be fine. It's OK." What I really thought was that he had absolutely planned this Christmas ski trip with his new girlfriend as some sort of victory lap — his way of reminding me that he was "winning" post-divorce.

"You're not just saying that to make me feel better, are you?" Of course I was! Lying was one of my top maternal skills. Right up there with guilt, and the mom death stare.

"No, of course not. You are an adult. And you get to decide how to spend your time. Things will always change - you may have kids of your own one day. You decide how you want to celebrate. You can't do it for someone else - there's no joy in that."

"OK Mom. Thanks." He was my easy child. I rarely felt the urge to pluck his eyelashes out one by one. Morgan was another story. I had to call her next, and fast before the buzz from the marg wore off.

"Hey, before you go, there is something I have been meaning to talk to you about." He hesitated, then added, "I wanted to talk about Katie. I'd like you to get to know her more. Maybe after the holidays we can all grab dinner? She's important to me, Mom."

That squeezed my heart in both directions at once. "If she's important to you, she's important to me," I said. "And dinner sounds perfect."

He exhaled like he'd been holding his breath. "Thanks, Mom."

"Of course. Good luck with the year-end sales push."

"You know it! Love you, Mom."

"Love you more."

◆ ◆ ◆

I dialed up Morgan next, and immediately regretted not having a second margarita. Oh well, here goes.

"Hey Mom, what's up." She answered like I was interrupting something important, which for Morgan could have been a surgical procedure or watching her nail polish dry.

"Not much sweetheart, are you busy?"

"No. I was just folding laundry."

"Well, that sounds thrilling."

"Mm-hmm. What's up?"

"Christmas," I said carefully.

"You can't change your mind now Mom. I already told him I would go with him…and that woman." She said it like she was being force-fed peas. Morgan hated peas.

"I'm not changing my mind. But you still seem upset about it. What's the problem?"

"I don't know why I have to spend time with her. I just think you and Dad are too old to be dating. These are your golden years. You should be playing bridge and eating dinner at 4."

I bit back a laugh. Bridge? The closest I'd come was once using a deck of Uno cards as coasters. And dinner at four? Please. That was happy hour.

This kid - she always knew just what to say to piss me off. She got that from her father.

"Listen Morgan. Your dad and I love you. Nothing will ever change that. But we both have a right to be happy. And if it makes your dad happy to be with whomever this person is, that's his prerogative. One day, I might meet someone, and that is my prerogative. You have only one choice in the matter - to suck it up. I guess you could choose to pout about it. But you don't get to choose for us." The best way to handle Morgan was tough love. She thrived on drama, but I refused to audition for her play.

"Like I told you yesterday, you are an adult. You can decide how you want to spend your time, and with whom. You don't owe me any apologies for choosing to go skiing. I think it will be a lot of fun, and I know your Dad will be happy to spend the time with you."

"OK. I just don't want to go and have them be all lovey dovey in front of me. It would be so awkward." I had no idea why she thought her dad was capable of "lovey dovey." The man treated public affection like a traffic violation. The only time he ever kissed me with more than just us in the room was on our wedding day — and even then, he looked like he was afraid he'd get fined for it.

"Awkward?" I said. "Like that time your dad and I caught you making out with the neighbor kid in the garage? Because that's still the reigning champ."

"Oh God Mom- why do you always bring that up?" Score one for Mom.

"Like I said- you need to put on your big girl panties. You can handle this. "

"Uhhh!" she groaned. In her language that was an agreement. "OK, fine."

"OK sweetheart. I'll talk to you next week. Love you."

"Love you."

An hour later, I was tucked into bed.

I thought the calls went well enough. There was only so much I could say. As much as I wanted to make everything okay for them, they'd have to figure that out themselves. It would take time. At least they'd get a guilt-free Christmas with their dad.

Now I just had to figure out how to make it okay for me. It hurt — I was angry, sad, and convinced my ex was making things harder on everyone, especially me. That was his specialty - one of the many reasons we divorced. And, damn it, I just did what I'd always done- covered for him, smoothed out the wrinkles he left behind.

He got the iron in the divorce. Why was I still on his emotional laundry duty? Time to retire from that job. Let him press his own shirts for once. Easy to say, harder to do— especially when the kids were involved. Maybe I'd always be protective, and maybe that was okay.

For now, though, the kids would be skiing for Christmas. And me? I'd be making my own run— straight down the slopes of solitude on Mount Solo.

Run club was rained out that week. But David and Disha met up with me for happy hour anyway. I told them both about the kids being with their Dad for Christmas.

"The holidays just feel weird now. We won't be doing the things we normally do. I'm going to miss having tacos for dinner and watching Christmas Vacation in our matching PJ's." Aaron always complained about the pajamas- he thought it was dumb. I supposed he wouldn't miss that, and I felt a little sadder. I was definitely complaining. Maybe whining, just a little. Who was I kidding, my pity party was as big as the Met Gala and in full swing.

"I know what you mean." David said. "Simon will be at his Mom's. I won't pick him up 'til later Christmas Day. I'll miss Christmas morning."

I had forgotten that David hadn't been divorced long either. It must be harder when your children are young, and Christmas is still a magical time.

"My family never celebrated Christmas. It was just a quiet day for us." Disha said. "But listen you guys, it will be what you make of it. It's just a new normal this year. You decide what that normal is. And it can still be great."

Disha was right. I liked the idea of a new normal. Since the divorce, very little from my old life was still part of my new life. Come to think of it, some parts of *me* were new too. I decided to embrace the "new normal" mindset.

"Cheers to that!" I said. And we clinked glasses.

"I have always wanted my house to be really decorated for Christmas. The works- lights outside, blow ups on the lawn, and a spectacular Christmas tree." David said.

Disha and I just stared at him. "Said no man ever." Disha chimed in. And we laughed.

"No, I mean it." He said, "I remember growing up, my parents decorated everything. Our house vomited Christmas- inside and out." You could tell he was recalling happy memories by how his face lit up.

"Then you should do it." I said, "What's stopping you?"

"I don't have a tree. And I am not sure what ornaments I got in the divorce. I just got what she gave me, which wasn't much," he said.

I took this as a personal challenge. My years of experience as the family Christmas Commander were about to get tested. I'd once micromanaged Christmas with the precision of a NASA launch. I was equal to the challenge.

"Ok, we have two hours before the stores close," I said, and I motioned for the waitress. "Let's go Christmas shopping."

We piled into David's car and headed to my favorite holiday decor warehouse — the kind of place that starts celebrating

Christmas in August. There were trees in every shape and color, aisles of coordinated ornaments, inflatable yard Santas the size of SUVs, and enough outdoor lights to land a plane.

When we walked in, David's face lit up like a kid on Christmas morning. I had never seen a man get that excited to shop or to decorate for Christmas. It was adorable. We convinced him to start with the tree. He chose a 7-foot tree with LED lights that twinkled in white or multi color.

"It helps if you have some kind of theme." I suggested.

"I just always loved how magical Christmas morning was. The excitement of Santa coming and leaving toys. I still feel that on Christmas morning. I know Santa's not real, but I kinda still believe he is."

Disha and I just stared at him. After a long beat, she said, "Okay, that's the most adorable thing I've ever heard. Who are you?"

We laughed, but David wasn't joking. His face was so open, so sincere.

My heart melted a little. This man wasn't just built for fatherhood—he still believed in the magic of childhood. And I got it. I never told my kids Santa wasn't real either. We kept the magic alive in our house as long as we could. We believed. Maybe I still did too.

I saw a tree skirt, and got my inspiration. I held it up- the word 'Believe' embroidered in white on the red skirt.

"What about this for a theme?"

Both Disha and David liked that idea, so the tree skirt went in the cart. He chose traditional Christmas colors-red, green, gold-and he really liked Santa's. By the time we checked out, all three of us were pushing carts.

We loaded up David's car. We were packed in like college students in an Uber on $1 margarita night.

We drove to David's place—a newer home just south of Denton, about the size of mine. The layout was great for entertaining- if one actually entertained.

It was clean in that post-divorced dad way: no dishes, just a lone coffee mug drying on the rack. Furniture was minimal and shoved against the walls like it had been afraid to settle in. No barstools, just a card table and two folding chairs in the dining area—he clearly got custody of the poker setup.

In the living room, a brown leather sofa and loveseat faced a TV so enormous I felt like I needed a neck brace and a ticket to the IMAX. A gaming console blinked beneath it—clearly for Simon, though the setup still had that temporary, just-passing-through energy.

The tree would need a spot, which meant the furniture would need to move—and probably stay moved. Never mind Feng Shui. We were going for Festive Functionality.

David went to grab what ornaments he did have from the attic.

"Hey Disha, let's move this around." I said, pointing to the living room.

"Gladly" she said.

I explained where I thought we should position things and she was fully onboard. By the time David returned with a large plastic tote, she and I had transformed the living room into a cozier space.

"Wow!" He sat and took in the room from a spot on the sofa. "I can see the TV better now." David said.

"I'm glad you like it. Let's see what you got." While David and I went through his ornaments, Disha started on the tree. David didn't have much- just the one box. But what he had was priceless: ornaments that Simon had made since he was little- stars from popsicles sticks, and bells from plastic cups. He also had quite a few that he'd made himself when he was a child. His

93

parents were gone, and he'd taken them when he cleaned out their things. They were so special, and would be perfect on his new tree.

There was one beautiful ornament made of delicate glass. It was painted white with red poinsettias, and green foliage. It was definitely old. David let me know it had been his Mother's favorite. I made a mental note to order an ornament stand for that one. It would be beautiful on the fireplace.

Once Disha had the tree assembled, we scooted it into place in front of the window—prime holiday real estate. I threaded ribbon through the branches while Disha and David unboxed ornaments like elves on a deadline. David found a Christmas music station—never mind that it was still a week before Thanksgiving-and blasted loud enough Santa could hear from the North Pole.

It was chaotic. It was cheerful. And somehow, it felt...kind of magical.

David placed the tree topper—the final touch—and flipped on the lights, now twinkling warm white. We collapsed onto the couch and admired our work, beaming like kids who just crushed their fifth-grade science fair.

It was beautiful- not in that sterile, department-store way, but in the way that matters. The tree was full of memories of people David loved. You could feel it.

David was clearly proud, and a little overcome. He put his arms around us, and hugged us both. "Thank you." He whispered.

It was after midnight by the time David drove us back to Moonwinks so we could get our cars.

I drove home in the quiet, feeling remarkably better than I'd felt since Monday. I was really happy that we could help David with his Christmas tree. It gave me hope for my own holiday, and some clarity, too.

Maybe I didn't need to be the Christmas Commander anymore. Maybe just showing up, helping someone else build their version of magic—that was enough.

Maybe, that's what I needed to do for my kids now-help *them* build their own version of magic. Maybe that's what I needed to do for myself.

Like Disha said, it would be normal. It would just be a *new* normal, and I got to decide what that would be.

CHAPTER 11

This year, my parents were hosting Thanksgiving—something they did every few years to remind themselves why they didn't do it every year. My youngest sister was coming up from Houston, and for the first time in forever, I wasn't splitting my time between two families. Just one turkey dinner this year. Only half the holiday bloat. I guess divorce is the new portion control.

It felt weird. A little melancholy. I used to bounce between my family and his, trying to make everyone happy while running on stuffing, pie and caffeine. It was exhausting.

I'd miss his family. I loved them. Twenty-five years is a long time to spend with people- it makes them yours, even when the marriage doesn't stick. I wondered if my family would miss him too. He was "Uncle T" to my nieces and nephews. My parents always liked him. We all lost something in the divorce, not just the marriage. I wondered how we could get some of it back. Maybe Tim and I had to be the ones to show everyone it was still okay to love us both.

Morgan, Aaron, and his girlfriend Katie would be joining us for an early Thanksgiving meal- early enough to eat before the Cowboys game, or what I like to call nap time. They planned to head to their dad's by halftime. I was just glad they were showing up at all.

I invited them to run the Turkey Trot with me, but neither seemed particularly thrilled about being upright before sunrise. Shocking.

I was pleasantly surprised when Morgan said she'd be getting off work early on Wednesday and wanted to stay the night at my house. I made up the guest room, stocked her favorite snacks, and crossed my fingers for a cozy mother-daughter moment watching the parade before we headed to my parents'. It would be the first time one of my kids had seen the new house.

After Amy and I got married (not to each other—though we probably would've had better luck), we started a tradition called Pie Wednesday. The night before Thanksgiving, we'd bake pies while eating pizza and pretending it was quality sister time— not hours of stress wrapped in a flaky crust. Over the years, it evolved into a casual drop-in party with friends, wine, and at least one of us throwing a pie crust on the floor.

This year, Amy was hosting again. I invited David and Disha. David had Simon for the week, and I told him to bring him— there were always plenty of kids running around. Run club was canceled for the holiday, so it seemed like the perfect night for chaos and carbs.

The Wednesday before the long shopping weekend finally arrived. I got off work at three, relaxed for a bit, then started gathering the things I needed to take to Amy's—pie plates, wine, and enough measuring cups to make us look competent.

Morgan arrived around five. I gave her the grand tour of the house- and introduced her to Prince. It was love at first bark. We took him for a walk, then tucked him into his crate like the royal he is and headed to Amy's around six.

Amy lived nearby in the house she and her husband bought when they were expecting Mattie. Big, bright, and basically built for holidays—with a real dining room, a home office, and a family room large enough to host a football team.

The kitchen opened into the living space with an island the size of a Smart Car and ceilings tall enough for a second Christmas tree. It was the kind of house where you could spill something and still feel welcome.

Upstairs, Mattie had taken over the old au pair suite. Now it was Teen Boy HQ—gaming setup, mini living room, full bathroom, and a couch that had probably never seen a vacuum. The kid was living the dream.

By 7:00, *Charlie Brown* was on, the pizza had arrived, and the house was buzzing. Amy and I were in our Thanksgiving aprons, alternating between rolling dough and topping off wine glasses.

Mom and Dad arrived with my youngest sister, Ellie. They didn't stay long—Mom had a turkey to brine —but Sharon stopped by too, and the two of them caught up in the kitchen like only dear friends can- whispering, laughing, hugging.

Disha, David, and Simon arrived not long after the pizza. Simon made a beeline upstairs with Mattie—apparently ten-year-olds speak the universal language of Roblox.

David, meanwhile, hovered. "What do I do?" he asked.

"You don't have to do anything. Just relax and enjoy yourself," I told him.

"But I came to bake pies," he said, already rolling up his sleeves.

"You don't have to ask me twice," Amy said, handing him a pile of apples and our terrifying-but-effective peeler.

"I'm good just watching," Disha added, glass of wine in hand, taking pictures like a proud stage mom.

Amy tied one of her frillier aprons around David—he didn't even flinch—and he dove in. And not just with enthusiasm—he actually knew what he was doing. He peeled, chopped, mixed, and measured like someone who had read a recipe *and* followed it. He helped roll out crust, shaped little leaves out of the extras for the top of the apple pie, and didn't blink when it was time to tackle dishes.

We worked well together—me, Amy, and David. We turned out a solid lineup: pumpkin, chocolate, Dad's favorite banana cream, and of course, apple. Amy and David bantered like they'd done this a dozen times. And I didn't mind sharing the kitchen-it was fun.

By the time the pies were cooling, the house felt full in the best kind of way: loud, warm, slightly sticky, and completely alive.

Everyone was gone by ten. It always worked that way. Thanksgiving was game day, and even a drop-in party had a curfew. Mattie had disappeared upstairs to his teenage cave, leaving just me, Amy, and Morgan in the kitchen.

Amy poured us each a glass of wine.

"Cheers to another Pie Wednesday," she said, holding up her glass.

"Cheers," I echoed.

Amy sipped, then asked casually, "How long have you known David?"

I shrugged. "A couple of months, I guess."

"He's really great."

I looked over at her, trying to read between the lines. Was she telling me *she* was interested? It wouldn't be the craziest idea—they got along, and he *was* great. I could picture it.

"Yeah. He's a great friend. They both are."

Amy glanced at me over the rim of her glass. "Have you ever thought about going out with him?"

Morgan stood up abruptly. "I'm gonna go check on Mattie," she said, and made a swift exit.

I blinked. "No! Of course not."

Amy tilted her head. "Why not?"

"I don't think of him like that. We're friends."

She didn't say anything, just raised an eyebrow.

"Besides," I added quickly, "I think there might be something going on with him and Disha. I'm not sure. They've never said anything, and I've never seen anything, but... I get a vibe."

"Hmmm."

"What?"

"I get a vibe too. But not about Disha."

I narrowed my eyes. "Amy..."

"I think he likes *you*."

I laughed- too quickly. "No. That's ridiculous. He's just nice. Your vibe is off."

But the second the words left my mouth, I felt a little off myself.

Later, as Morgan and I drove home, the question crept back in.

Did David like me?

And more dangerous: did *I* like *him*?

I tried to swat the thought away, but it buzzed around my brain like one of those annoying fruit flies that shows up the second you forget to rinse the wine glass.

Okay, so maybe we had a connection. Of sorts. He was comfortable. Easy. The kind of person you could talk to about anything and somehow end up laughing at nothing. But I wasn't letting myself go there. He was a friend- mine, and Disha's.

That's all it was.

Probably.

And I had zero plans to ever date again. Ever. I had made that very clear.

Still… I wondered what Amy saw that I didn't. That would keep me awake a night or two.

I pulled into the driveway and made myself a deal: I would not overthink it. I would not spiral. I would not Google "signs your friend is secretly into you."

I would put it out of my head. Go forward, resolve intact.

And I would sleep like a baby.

Probably

Thanksgiving morning was brutally cold with the temperature hovering around the freezing mark. It was overcast and threatened to rain. A Turkey Trot was being held in several locations around the metroplex. Our running group was doing one in Denton at the College.

I dressed as warmly as possible, never having run in weather this cold before. I grabbed my turkey hat-everyone in the run club got one for the race. I threw on some colorful knee socks over my yoga pants. I looked a little silly, but that's what I was going for.

I arrived at the college, and nothing could have prepared me for the arctic wind that punched me in the face the second I got out of the car. As I walked toward the registration tables, all I could think about was my flannel jammies, a fleece blanket, and a coffee mug big enough to hide behind. Preferably while not doing this.

I met up with David and Simon at the registration table. Disha had opted out—said it was too cold and sent a very early text to let us know. Smart girl. I just wish she'd told me bailing was an option *before* I pried myself out of bed.

Pete showed up too—and did not disappoint. He was dressed in a full-blown inflatable turkey costume, complete with flapping wings and an unsettlingly cheerful beak. It was hysterical. Pete didn't just show up—he *committed*.

While we waited for the race to start, he strutted around the crowd gobbling at people and waving at frozen, giggling children like some deranged poultry parade marshal.

"Good morning for a run!" David joked.

"I'm warm!" Said Pete. His air-filled costume must have been good insulation.

"Are you a runner too, Simon?" I asked. He seemed to still be half asleep.

"Yes, ma'am." He replied with a yawn.

I suggested that I could run with Simon, and David could run at his usual pace.

"Is that ok with you, son." David asked Simon.

"Yes, sir."

It was settled. We took our places at the starting line, and the race started.

Simon was fast. I, unfortunately, wasn't. I managed to keep up—for the first quarter mile. Then the sleet started. By the half-mile, it was coming down sideways and slapping us in the face. Simon looked miserable. I probably looked like a damp scarecrow sprinting after a child.

"You ok, Simon?"

"Yes, ma'am. I'm just really cold. I wish we could have stayed home and had cinnamon rolls."

I nodded, sleet coating my eyelashes. "You had cinnamon rolls?"

He shook his head. "No. But we *could* have."

Fair point.

"Hey kiddo. I'm really cold. I think we should stop. Is that ok?"

"Yes, Ma'am." He seemed relieved.

"We can wait for your dad in my car and get warm. Sound good?"

"Yes, ma'am."

I texted David. I wasn't sure Simon would be cool going to my car, but one message from Dad and all that 'Stranger Danger' training went right out the frosty window.

We turned around and made a beeline for the parking lot, huddling together like two underdressed penguins in a sleet storm. Once in the car, I cranked the heater like we were trying to roast a turkey in the front seat.

I got a text from David.

David: *I gave up too. Way too cold. Meet me at Brew House, and I'll buy you a coffee for watching Si.*

Me: Sounds wonderful. Will Simon be ok with me leaving with him?

David: I'll text him and he'll be fine.

We made our way over to the coffee shop. There was no one there, and I was a little surprised they were even open. But happy- very happy. The three of us sat with our warm drinks, and pumpkin pastries as the feeling slowly returned to my extremities.

"Thank you for letting us come over last night, Ms. Renee." Offered Simon.

"You are welcome anytime."

"Mattie had some fun games. I liked the one where you can build stuff."

I had no idea what that was. I wasn't a video gamer. For all I knew, he could've been constructing a treehouse... or a flamethrower. Hard to say with these games.

We laughed at some of the crazy costumes we saw, but agreed that Pete's was the best. We didn't stay long. We all had places to be- I needed to get home to watch the parade with Morgan, and they were going to David's brothers. The boys hugged me, and wished me a Happy Thanksgiving, and I headed home.

Despite the weather, it had been a surprisingly nice morning. David and Simon were just so... easy. Easy to talk to, easy to be around. No pressure. No drama. No pretending to be something you're not.

For a fleeting moment, I let myself wonder what it would be like- *really* be like- with David.

And then I yanked myself back to reality like a kid caught snooping for presents. No. I wasn't dating anyone. Things were finally feeling normal again- comfortable, consistent. My life had just stopped spinning. Why on earth would I toss a wrench into that?

Still, as I drove home with the heat blasting and the smell of pumpkin pastry clinging to my jacket, I couldn't help but think-

My resolve was... maybe a little frostbitten.

Thanksgiving felt more normal than I expected. We ate and had the dishes done before kick-off. We watched the Cowboys play, and napped. Then later, we ate turkey sandwiches and played games. It was a wonderful day.

On Saturday, I decided to start decorating my house for

Christmas. Morgan came over and helped me.

As we opened boxes, I thought about how little David had for decorations-just the one small box. I realized that I had gotten all of the Christmas decorations, and felt selfish for leaving my ex with nothing.

"Morgan, help me pick out some things for your dad. He should have some of this."

"Ok." She seemed happy about that idea.

We chose some ornaments that reminded us of him, and some other decorations that I didn't need or have a place for, and put them in some boxes. As a joke, I included the dancing Snoopy dressed like Santa- when you pushed the button on his foot, he would wiggle his behind to Feliz Navidad. I always teased Tim that he danced like that. Morgan agreed to take them to him.

I realized that I could do this-share the kids, my family, and Christmas ornaments with Tim. I could still love him, and not be married to him. We could be a family without being a couple. I felt lighter, and consoled. Any lingering pain I felt over the divorce felt lessened. I decided not to hang on to hurt, anger or resentment.

I chose to love.

CHAPTER 12

With Thanksgiving behind me, I set my sights on Christmas. I had a lot of shopping, baking, and mailing to do in just three short weeks. I was doing my best to enjoy all the delights of the season without thinking too hard about how alone I'd be on the actual day. I listened to the music, watched the movies, and baked the cookies- channeling Martha Stewart. But there was still a bit of sadness lurking just underneath it all.

Like salt in a wound, my company's Christmas dinner was in two weeks. The president hosted a fancy dinner downtown for the leadership team and their partners at a nice restaurant— the kind with a dress code and jackets required. It really was a generous gesture, and I'd always enjoyed the event in the past. But this year, having neither a spouse nor a significant other, I'd be attending alone. I wanted to skip it, but that would've been the political equivalent of lighting myself on fire and handing out marshmallows.

It was the first Wednesday after Thanksgiving, and I skipped run club. It was too cold to run. I stayed in and did laundry. I'd decided I wouldn't run outside if the temperature was under 50 degrees. The Turkey Trot had done me in. I saw no reason to freeze my jingle bells off.

I got texts from David, Disha, Pete, and Ashley—all checking in to make sure I was okay. Such good friends.

Disha texted again the following Monday to remind me that the run club would have a holiday get-together this week after the Wednesday run. We'd be exchanging white elephant gifts. I promised her I'd be there.

Two days later, it was still hovering in the too-cold zone, but I ran anyway. I hadn't realized how much better I felt when I ran regularly. I was still slower than Disha and David, and I had no delusions about ever catching up with Ashley. But I was keeping pace with several others now. I rarely ran alone.

As always, David circled back and ran the rest of the distance with me— though the loop was much shorter now than when I'd first started in September.

"This cold's not scaring you off?" he asked, matching my pace.

"Nope. I've decided I'm either committed or I've lost all sense of reason. Not sure which yet."

He laughed. "Maybe a little of both."

When we reached the finish, he rested his hand lightly on my back for just a moment, guiding me toward the door. "Come on— warmth and beer await."

It was nothing, really. Just a friendly gesture. But it felt... steady. Easy. And at the same time, it was something else too — something I didn't want to think about yet.

Tonight, run club met in a different room on Moonwinks' second floor set up for private events — one less flight of stairs to climb. Thank you, Santa. Disha had decorated and laid out trays of hors d'oeuvres like we were about to run a 10K in evening wear. A cash bar stood in the corner. Of course, Disha had found sponsors to cover the room and food — because apparently she's part event planner, part magician.

David and I joined the line for the bar, shuffling forward as people ahead of us placed their orders. The room was packed — at least fifty people, including some I'd never seen at the group runs. David told me some were spouses and others just came for the parties.

When we reached the front of the line, he leaned toward me. "What are you having?"

"Cabernet," I said. "Unless they have something that will make me forget the stairs."

He smirked. "Two Cabernets, then."

We stepped aside with our drinks, letting the next round of thirsty runners take our place. David handed me mine without spilling a drop — a minor miracle in a room this crowded. We found a spot with a decent view of the room, close enough to catch snippets of conversation and people-watch.

That's when I saw Pete — dressed like the elf from that popular Christmas movie. We could always count on Pete to bring the fun.

And it was no longer a question— Scott and Ashley were definitely dating. They were holding hands now.

Disha stepped up to a mic connected to a small speaker. After getting everyone's attention, she smiled. "Happy Holidays! And welcome to the Denton Running and Walking Club!"

Everyone cheered.

"I want to thank our event sponsors—Denton Running Shoe Co., County Orthopedics, and of course, Moonwinks."

Applause.

"I have something for you if you come see me after the party," she added, nodding to a box behind her. run club t-shirts. She was a marketing genius.

"A couple of quick announcements, and then we'll start the gift exchange. I know you're all dying to see what amazing treasures you'll win." A few people chuckled. The price limit was five dollars, and Disha had said it was totally fine to re-gift. I brought a Christmas candle I'd gotten from a neighbor the year before.

"Run club will be suspended until the second week in January. You're welcome to still meet up here and enjoy Moonwinks, but officially we're on holiday break."

She continued, "The Cowtown Marathon is coming up in February. Anyone training for that, we've got a Saturday morning group forming. We'll meet at 6 a.m. at Funky Fusion Coffee just up the road. Delilah, the owner, is here—raise your hand, Delilah! She's offering 10% off pastries with coffee purchase after the run. Thank you, Delilah—I've got something for you, too."

More applause.

"That's it—who's ready to play?"

Only about 25 people joined the white elephant game. When it was over, Disha had a lovely crocheted scarf. I ended up with a coffee mug covered in dogs wearing Christmas hats, filled with chocolate kisses. David definitely won the weirdest gift—he got a jar of belly button lint, courtesy of Pete. I made a mental note to step up my gift game next year.

Afterward, David and I helped Disha clean up, then the three of us found a table downstairs at the bar.

"That was really fun, Disha. Great job!"

"Cheers to that," David said, raising his glass.

"Thanks, guys," she replied.

"So, what are you doing for Christmas?" I asked her.

She told me her family didn't celebrate Christmas. "I've done different things in the past. Not sure what I'll do this year."

I already knew David would be seeing Simon later on Christmas Day, but I didn't know about the rest of his plans. I thought he had a brother nearby.

"What about you?" I asked David.

"I have no plans until I pick up Simon."

I got the sense he was struggling too with how to spend the day alone.

"Hey! I should be done with church by six. Let's go to dinner—the three of us—on Christmas Eve." I know a few restaurants that stay open. I'm sure we could find something.

"Yes! Let's do that," Disha said.

"I'm in," David added, sounding a bit more cheerful.

"Yes! This will be fun. Now if I could just get out of my work dinner." I hadn't meant to say that part out loud.

"What's that about?" Disha asked.

"Oh. Every year, we have this dinner at Reata in Fort Worth."

"Ooo. Fancy."

"It really is. The president pays for it out of his own pocket—steak, fish, open bar."

"So, what's the problem?" David asked.

"It's going to sound dumb, but I think I'll be the only one there flying solo. I'm just not sure I'm up for it."

"Take me," David said — like it was no big deal.

"Take you?" I repeated, unsure if he was joking or just really committed to steak.

"What kind of friend would I be if I let you go alone to a work dinner? Especially one with steak and an open bar? I'll be your plus one."

Okay, so he was being a good friend. I should've felt relief. So why did it feel... complicated?

"Take David," Disha chimed in. "You guys will have a great time."

"I mean, if you want to- sure. Why not? Thanks."

And just like that, I had a plus one for my work dinner. And plans for Christmas Eve.

David was the first to leave. Disha and I stayed, finishing our sodas.

"So hey, is it really okay that David goes with me to the work dinner?"

She gave me a curious look. "Of course. Why wouldn't it be?"

"Honestly, I've never asked, but I wasn't sure what the nature of your relationship with David is. If there's something there, I don't want to overstep."

Disha laughed. "No. David and I are just friends. I'm gay, Renee."

"Oh." Should she have told me that before? I don't go around announcing I'm straight, so why would she? Was I supposed to ask? I hoped I hadn't been a bad friend by not knowing. I just hoped she knew I didn't care. Or- I cared *about her*- just not who she dated. Wait, that sounded wrong too. She was an amazing person, and I cared that she found someone who treated her well. Nothing I could say would sound quite right, so I said nothing.

"In my culture, sex is rarely discussed. And people like me aren't accepted. I haven't even told my parents."

"I'm sorry." As a mother, I hoped my kids knew they could be their authentic selves, and I'd love them fiercely. "I wish I had known sooner. I could've been screening dates for you all year."

"Maybe that's why I didn't tell you sooner." She winked.

"So," I said, changing gears, "do you have plans for Christmas Day?"

"No. What are you thinking?"

We ended up pulling out our phones, scrolling through "Things to do Christmas Day" like we were planning a heist. By the time we were done, we had Christmas brunch at the Gaylord, tickets to the ICE! exhibit, and a movie to close it out.

I drove home feeling lighter than I had in weeks.

I had plans for Christmas that didn't involve me eating an entire roll of uncooked cookie dough, crying, or watching Home Alone.

I had a plus one for my work dinner—and a good one at that.

And most of all, I had people in my life who made the season feel full again.

This "new normal" had started to feel… pretty wonderful.

CHAPTER 13

It was the Saturday of my office Christmas dinner. I had just walked in from yoga when David texted me.

David: You busy today?

Me: Loaded question. Why? If you need help moving, then yes, I'm busy.

David: Ha ha. No, but I need a woman's opinion.

Me: OK. I have those in spades.

David: I knew I came to the right place. Go shopping with me?

Me: Shopping? That's like my superpower.

David: I'm on my way.

Me: Slow down—need 30 minutes.

David: Ok.

Still sweaty from yoga, I showered and changed into my standard shopping uniform—clean yoga pants, sweater, cute sneakers. My new rule was that running shoes were only for running. I had just let Prince back in the house when the doorbell rang.

Prince did his usual—charging the door barking, then spinning frantic little circles until I opened it.

I let David in, and he bent to greet Prince. "Hey, buddy. Aren't you a cutie?"

Usually, Prince barked until he'd sized someone up. But this time

—nothing. He jumped up on David, tail wagging, like he'd been waiting his whole life for him to show up. No suspicion, no hesitation- just instant approval.

It was…odd. Prince liked him. Immediately.

We left a few minutes later, Prince tucked in his crate. David drove.

"So, what are we shopping for?" I asked.

"I need a shirt to wear with my suit tonight. Maybe a new tie."

I felt guilty—he was doing this for me.

"I need them for work anyway," he added. Maybe to make me feel better. Only attorneys and undertakers wore suits to work anymore. I was pretty sure his uniform as a software engineer was T-shirts and sweatpants.

We pulled into a shopping center, and David steered us towards a menswear store.

I loved a good menswear store. It gave the illusion that men were stylish, well-dressed creatures. In reality, I knew from twenty-five years of marriage this was a fairy tale. Tim had exactly four pairs of work slacks- khaki, dark khaki, navy, and black- which covered him Monday through Thursday. Fridays were jeans and polos. He owned one funeral suit, which I was pretty sure could now only be worn by a slimmer, younger man—or possibly a slightly paunchy mannequin.

David, on the other hand, I'd only ever seen in running gear or jeans. But I could tell he cared about the details- like his hands. Nice hands. Nails short and clean. The kind of hands that told you this man did not, for example, use a butter knife as a screwdriver.

We were greeted by an older gentleman in slacks, a vest, and bow tie. I think he introduced himself as Jim, but in my head, he was instantly "Dapper Dan." David told him his shirt size, and Dapper

Dan swept us over to a wall of neatly folded shirts, handing David several before disappearing to the dressing rooms with him like a haberdashery fairy godmother.

Left alone, I wandered toward the ties. My dress for tonight was deep green, and without thinking, I started looking for something that would match. Then I caught myself. What was I doing? Was I... matching? Coordinating? Did I think we were going to walk in holding hands like the prom royalty of the Fort Worth Leadership Team? Would they hand us a crown and sash between the soup and the salad course? Oh God, was I about to become *that* woman- the one who pretends she's "just friends" while color-matching her plus one? I took two quick steps away from the tie rack as if it might file a restraining order.

David emerged in a beige shirt. It fit his shoulders, but the waist was loose enough to smuggle a family of squirrels.

"I think you need the athletic cut," I said.

Dapper Dan reappeared, nodding in agreement. He and I grabbed a few more shirts, and he handed them over to David.

"Your husband is in great shape," he said.

"Oh, he's not my husband. We run together."

Dapper Dan froze, then gave me a slow nod.

Run together—did that mean something else in bow-tie land?

When David came back out in a crisp white shirt that fit perfectly, I wasn't drooling. Probably. But I did think the store thermostat might have been set to "tropical."

"This one better?" he asked.

"That works." And it did. *Really* well.

He emerged from the dressing room a few minutes later, shirt in hand.

"I need a tie," he said. "All of mine are old."

"How old? Maybe they're back in style."

He ignored me, and we walked to the tie display. "What color are you wearing?"

It took me a second to answer because- wait- he was thinking about matching too?

"Uh, deep green. Like this," I said, pointing to a tie with just a hint of the color woven in.

We stood there, side by side, flipping through ties until we settled on one. It was a quiet, subtle match. The kind of thing no one else might notice- but I did.

We were checking out when he asked, "You hungry?"

"I am."

"Let's grab lunch."

We found a Mexican place nearby. Lunch was easy, familiar- margaritas, laughter, and me pretending the second margarita was "just to keep him company" instead of "because it's Saturday and I have no self-control and like a good skinny marg." By three- o'clock, not margs- I needed to get ready for the dinner, and possibly grab a quick nap, so we headed home.

"Thanks for your help today," he said when we pulled up. "I'll be back by 6:30. We'll grab an Uber."

"Perfect. I'll see you then"

I was smiling when I walked in. It could've been from the two margaritas. Could've been that I spent the afternoon with someone whose company I enjoyed, who made me feel good- light in a way I'd not felt in a long time. It was always easy around David- to be just me without apology, or filter.

It was perfect.

Now all I had to do was not overthink the next three hours before he came back. Magic 8 ball said *Unlikely*.

I was looking forward to the dinner more than I wanted to admit. In the past, Tim had come along, but not so much *with* me as *alongside* me—like a coat that gets hung on the back of your chair unless it's cold or time to leave.

David was different. At run club, he talked to everyone- new people, old members, random dog walkers passing by. He remembered names, asked questions, and actually listened to the answers. I'd seen him make strangers feel like they belonged in the space of thirty seconds. That gave me hope about tonight. If anyone could make a stuffy work dinner bearable, it was him.

David arrived ten minutes early- handsome in a suit, holding a large wrapped box. My heart skipped. Or maybe tripped over itself. Either way, it was embarrassing.

"Wow, you clean up good," I teased.

"You, too. You look beautiful."

And there it was- blushing. Fabulous.

"This is for the toy drive," he said.

"Wow, that's thoughtful."

"I hate the thought of a kid not having anything for Christmas."

I thought I had my heart locked in a safe, secured with multifactor authentication- the kind that texts you a code and makes you swear an oath- but somehow it melted anyway.

"I'll order the car." And I grabbed my phone. I hoped he didn't notice how flustered I was.

"I already got one. It will be here at 6:30."

"Oh. Thank you."

I grabbed my coat from the hall closet. David took it from me, and helped me put it on. I grabbed my package for the toy drive, and David took it from me also. I had a feeling it was going to be a long night.

◆ ◆ ◆

David was an absolute gentleman- holding car doors, helping me out of the car- his manners were swoon-worthy. The attention made me feel special and valued in a way I had not realized I was missing.

The restaurant was beautiful- festive lighting, a giant Christmas tree, soft music. David didn't just stand there like a plus-one prop- he *showed up.* He chatted with my coworkers like he'd known them for years. He asked Carter about his marathon training, complimented Linda's hideous-but-memorable holiday sweater, and even laughed at Carl from accounting's joke about depreciation (which was proof enough he deserved sainthood).

It was almost too easy to imagine what it would be like if he really were my date. Which was dangerous. Because friends were safe. Friends didn't break your heart. And I wasn't sure I could survive another round of that.

When we left, David retrieved our coats, holding mine as I slipped it on. Over my shoulder, I caught Mr. Chase noticing- and nodding in approval. Outside, the chill nudged us shoulder to shoulder. We stood close while waiting for the car, the heat from his shoulder seeping through my coat.

It was late, and between the wine and the hour, I felt suddenly tired. The hum of the car and the quiet between us made it worse- or better, depending on how you looked at it. I'd had enough wine to blur the edges of my restraint. "Is it okay if I lay my head on your leg?" I asked.

"Sure."

He rubbed my head gently-the kind of touch that would make any cat purr and any woman melt.

We got to my house, and David's ride wasn't there yet. I invited him to wait inside, out of the cold. I felt like I had sobered up enough on the ride to be in full control now.

He came in and sat down. I offered him water, and grabbed two bottles from the fridge.

I sat on the couch, close- but not too close. We were both quiet. That was odd for us.

But I made a decision.

I was going to ask him.

I was going to ask if he'd ever thought about us. About maybe going on a real date.

Just once.

I was going to do it.

Here I go.

Silence.

Heavy. Bearing down on me. Holding back the question that hovered at the edge of my lips, burning for release.

I couldn't speak.

I couldn't move.

From the outside, we probably looked like two friends winding down after a long night - sipping water, not saying much. Tired perhaps. It was late after all.

Inside, my heart was racing and at war with my head.

The words twisted in my chest, coiled tight in fear, and sank like a stone.

I couldn't look at him. Couldn't look away either.

The silence stretched, brittle and deafening- a mocking reminder of my weakness.

The only sound in the house was the low hum of the refrigerator.

Steady. Unbothered.

As if I hadn't just decided to throw myself off a cliff from which there was no return.

I felt my heart fracture at the realization that I couldn't.

I just couldn't.

I was afraid.

What if he hadn't thought about it? What if he didn't want me?

What if he never would?

I just wasn't ready to go through that again.

I wasn't strong enough yet to survive another *no*.

Not from someone who mattered.

It could've been minutes or hours.

The silence pressed from all sides-suffocating and final.

Then I heard the faint buzz from David's phone.

"Car's here. I should get going."

"Of course." I offered him a wan smile, and walked him to the door.

"David, thank you, really, for going with me. It was so nice of you."

"It was my pleasure," he said. "Good night."

And he left.

That night I lay in bed and let that little voice say, I told you so. I should've kept my boundaries. Stopped imagining things could be different. I clearly wasn't up for that. I wasn't ready — not now, not when I was just starting to like the person I was becoming.

So, I sealed up every crack in my resolve, patched over the soft spots, and went to sleep.

I wasn't ready — for any of it.

CHAPTER 14

Christmas week marked the last run club meet until the new year. I skipped it. It was on the cusp of being too cold. But truthfully—I wasn't avoiding the cold. I was avoiding David. I wasn't ready to face him, or the small matter of not being brave enough to try.

I got texts from Ashley, Pete, and Disha. No text from David. Which was fine. Totally fine. I mean, I hardly noticed. Except I did. And it cut in a way I didn't want to admit.

On Christmas Eve, I worked a half day—wrapping gifts while monitoring my team's chat channel. The kids wouldn't be back until Monday, so we planned to connect the following Saturday. I had extra time to get ready, which mostly meant wandering around the house pretending I had important things to do. Normally I'd take my tree down right after Christmas, but I was "embracing the new normal," so it stayed up until we were officially done celebrating. My tree and I were rebels now.

Disha texted both David and me, checking on our dinner plans.

I sent back a dancing reindeer gif, because nothing says "I'm fine" like a badly animated deer in a Santa hat. I was relieved when David responded too.

David: Time and place?

Disha: 6:30? Amigos Cocina?

David: Works.

Me: Another reindeer gif, because apparently that's who I am now.

I'd reconciled my feelings about David—or boxed them up, labeled them "Do Not Open," and shoved them into the farthest corner of the attic in my head. I convinced myself our friendship was more valuable than a date, and that I just needed to go back to how it was before. That was the plan. I was holding to it like a woman clinging to the last brownie at a potluck.

I decided to go to mass at 3:30, which meant arriving by 2:30 if I wanted a seat. Any other Sunday, the place was a third full. But Christmas and Easter? Standing room only. No Catholic would miss church for the birth or the resurrection — that's double the penance of skipping a regular Sunday, maybe even fast-track-to-purgatory territory.

In recent years, the parish had started hosting a Christmas carol sing-along from 2:30 to 3, so people arriving early wouldn't get bored. Honestly, it was a nice touch.

Right at noon, the team chat started dinging. The few people still working were logging off, but not before wishing everyone a Merry Christmas. Then I saw a private message from Carter.

Car Johnson: Merry Christmas! Let's do lunch after the new year. Hugs.

Ren Masters: Merry Christmas and my best to Devon. Lunch for sure.

Car Johnson: Give that hunky David my best. You have some things to tell me about.

I just left that there. I'd explain when I saw him—later.

I had a little time before mass. After a quick lunch of peanut butter on a rice cake, I called my parents to make sure they'd made it safely to my brother's. I'd text the kids tomorrow so I wouldn't disturb their time with their dad.

At 2:00, I drove to church. The wind had a bite to it, sharp enough to find the gap between my scarf and coat. Families moved around me—toddlers in frilly Christmas dresses and little suits, patent leather shoes clacking on the pavement; teens looking mildly horrified to be wearing "dressy" clothes. The air carried the faint smell of chimney smoke, the tinny ring of a bell from somewhere down the street, and the sweet trace of sugar cookies drifting from the vestibule.

Joy practically hummed in the cold air, buzzing from the kids who were brimming with anticipation about Christmas morning.

And just like that, the thin little shield I'd been propping myself up with all day cracked. The cold went straight through me. My chest felt hollow.

Suddenly, I felt so brutally alone.

I missed my own kids, who always attended church with me for Christmas. I missed that feeling, that magic that had always been part of Christmas Eve since I was a child. I felt like it was gone.

And I wasn't sure I'd ever feel it again.

The sanctuary was quiet when I walked in. It always was before mass- a time set aside for quiet prayer and reflection.

Today, the silence was almost suffocating.

It pressed against me- a constant reminder of my alone-ness.

I usually sat in the middle, but today I chose the last pew in the back, closest to the door. It felt safer there, somehow. Easier to disappear.

A much older gentleman slid into the pew beside me. He smiled kindly as he settled in, and I nodded back with a faint smile of my own.

At 2:30, someone stepped forward and led Christmas carols. The songs were familiar, the voices warm and joyous.

I couldn't bring myself to sing.

I searched for any thread of joy I could hold onto.

But my soul felt still, quiet.

Empty.

The singing ended, the church fell silent again.

I watched as the man knelt slowly. With a rosary in his hand, he bowed his head and prayed, touching bead by bead as he completed his offering. Then he slowly returned to his seat beside me.

Mass began. The music was beautiful and moving. The familiar cadence of the service and the prayers brought a quiet comfort-like when I was little and my dad would wrap me in his arms.

The homily was short. We got to the part of the service where we recited the Lord's prayer. On instinct, I held out my hand. My family and I always held hands during the Lord's prayer. Before I realized what I'd done, the man took my hand, he laid his other hand on my shoulder and prayed.

"Our Father…"

I knew deep inside that he wasn't praying with me- he was praying for me. I couldn't stop the tears that had been threatening to overwhelm me since I'd walked in, or maybe they had been there for much longer, waiting.

I finally let them go.

They were tears of mourning, acceptance, and profound gratitude.

I'd had an incredible journey over the last year. I'd felt alone more times than I could count. Every time when I felt it couldn't possibly get any darker, someone would show up and bring the light.

Whether it was Amy, my running group friends, and even this

stranger. Someone always showed up.

When mass ended, all I had left was joy and gratitude. I hugged the man, and wished him a merry Christmas.

I left, not with answers, but with peace. And for the first time in a long time, that was enough.

CHAPTER 15

I walked out of church like a great weight had been lifted. When I got into my car, I grabbed my phone and saw I had missed several calls from Morgan and Aaron- well, make that one call from Aaron, four calls from Morgan- as well as a text that said "Call me ASAP."

I was more curious than worried. If it were truly an emergency, Aaron would likely have called multiple times. Getting multiples from Morgan could have meant either that the world was coming to an end, or her favorite TV show was.

I started the car, and headed home.

"Hey Siri, Call Morgan"

"Calling Morgan"

Morgan picked up immediately.

"Oh my God Mom, where have you been?"

"Church, sweetheart. What's up?"

"Mom, you will never believe this."

"What?" This was Morgan's way. She never just told you. There was always a dramatic build and then she dropped the bomb.

"So, you know how we are supposed to be on our way to New Mexico?"

Uh oh. "Yes..."

I could hear Aaron in the background now. "Just tell her, Morgan!"

"So, Dad and his girlfriend got in a fight, and now we are NOT going to New Mexico. We are just sitting at Dad's. He has been in the other room on the phone all day."

I felt bad for the kids. And a little for Tim. Just a little-microscopically small.

So little, in fact that I let myself relish his pain for just a minute. There really is a Santa Claus!

I knew that when I replied to Morgan, I had to be the bigger person. Here goes nothing.

"I am really sorry to hear that, sweetheart." I am seriously good at this.

"We are coming over. We want to eat food and watch Christmas movies. We have to come back to Dad's tonight. He wants us to stay there. He says he is making us a nice breakfast tomorrow."

"Sweetie, you are welcome to come to the house, but I have dinner plans. I should only be gone a few hours." I had considered cancelling to be with the kids, but truth be told, I didn't want to.

"Ok, we're coming then."

"Thanks Mom." I heard Aaron yell in the background.

I had a little time before dinner with Disha and David, so I took Prince for a walk and gave myself a pep talk along the way. I didn't want there to be any weirdness tonight. I wanted it to be easy. Fun. Like it had always been.

By the time I got home, I felt more grounded. Resolute. Armed and ready for a festive evening. I touched up the makeup I'd cried off at church and decided to take a page from *The Book of Pete*: I put on a ridiculous Christmas sweater—bright red with a giant blinking reindeer—leggings, and ankle boots. I left a key under the mat for Aaron and Morgan, then headed to Amigos Cocina.

The restaurant was moderately busy, but the wait was only fifteen minutes.

Disha arrived first.

"Merry Christmas," we said, hugging.

"I thought we said no gifts?" she asked, eyeing the bags in my hand.

"I thought we did too," I pointed to the ones in hers.

We were laughing when David walked in.

He looked… really good. Jeans, boots, a blue quarter-zip sweater over a henley that made his eyes look even bluer. I groaned inwardly. This might be harder than I thought.

"Hey- I thought we said no gifts?" he smiled, holding up two small packages.

We all laughed.

He hugged us both and wished us a Merry Christmas. And *damn it*, why did he have to smell so good too?

The hostess called our name, and we followed her to a booth. Disha and I slid into a side before I realized- I'd left David to choose. Would he sit by me? For half a second, I thought he might. But then he slid in beside Disha, smiling easily, like it was the most natural thing in the world. Maybe it was. Still, the tiniest sting slipped in before I pushed it away.

The waiter appeared with chips and salsa and took our drink orders. We raised our glasses.

"To friendship and Christmas," Disha said, lifting her margarita.

"Merry Christmas," we echoed.

Maybe it was because Disha was there, or maybe because we all needed this to feel normal- but soon we were laughing and chatting like always. It was easy again. Familiar. Comfortable.

The dishes were cleared, and we all decided to splurge on dessert. As we waited for our sopapillas, Disha handed us each a gift bag.

"I hope you like it," she said.

She'd gotten us small handheld water bottles, designed to be carried on a run. I'd been using a clunky old water bottle. This was way better.

We thanked her, and I passed over my gifts. Disha opened a motivational desk calendar for runners.

David unwrapped a Christmas ornament—two little elves, one taller, one smaller. I'd had their names added: *David* and *Simon*. The year was etched in the corner.

It felt a little too personal the moment he held it in his hands. But I wanted him to know I saw him- not just as my friend, but as a father trying to give his son the same magic and memories of Christmas that he cherished.

He smiled when he saw it and looked up at me- *really* looked at me- for the first time that evening.

"Thank you," he said softly.

David went last. He handed us each a small box from a jewelry store I knew well. Inside mine was a silver beaded bracelet with a crystal-inlaid heart charm. Disha's was gold with an octagonal iridescent stone. We slipped them on immediately.

"It's beautiful," I said, glancing up at him.

"Thank you," Disha added, leaning over to kiss his cheek.

We finished dessert and walked together into the cold parking lot. Quick hugs, promises to text soon, and we went our separate ways.

As I headed to my car, I felt something I couldn't quite name—a mix of gratitude and regret. The evening had been lovely. Light. Easy.

But also…

I kept letting something walk away, and I wasn't sure how many more times I could do that before I lost it altogether.

◆ ◆ ◆

I walked in the door at about 9:30. Nothing could have prepared me for what I found.

It was a scene straight out of a Hallmark Christmas movie—warm and sappy.

Except…

There.

In *my* chair.

Tim.

Tim was in my chair—his feet propped up on *my* ottoman, snuggled in *my* new throw blanket like some kind of reformed suburban housecat.

And on the side table?

My new dog mug.

Did he seriously use *my* new dog mug?

What. The. Actual. Hell.

Did I miss something in the divorce settlement?

How did *I* end up with custody of Tim for Christmas this year?

The kids finally realized I had come in and looked up briefly.

"Hey Mom." Then turned their attention back to the movie they had seen a gazillion times- like there was nothing unusual about their Dad sitting in their Mom's living room.

Morgan. She said "we" are coming over. I assumed she meant she and her brother. But she really meant "we". I'm glad they were so comfortable, but really?

Tim stood up and walked over to me.

"Hey Renee. I hope it's OK that I'm here. Merry Christmas." He reached out and hugged me.

Tim looked like he'd gone ten rounds in an MMA ring. Maybe he was struggling with a new normal like the rest of us. Seeing him like that didn't give me the smug satisfaction I was expecting. It just made me want to be kinder than I'd planned. Not kind enough to share my new dog mug, but I'd let him use my blanket.

There was Tim, there was me, and there was "us" — what Tim and I were together. Maybe, like me, Tim had lost a little of who he was outside of us. Maybe he too was still figuring that out.

And then there was our family. Different now, but still ours. If that meant Tim sitting in my living room on Christmas Eve, then maybe that was worth holding onto.

"You are welcome any time."

He plopped himself back in my chair, and watched the movie. I plugged the Christmas tree in and sat on the couch. I watched the movie for a bit, taking in the scene around me- my weird and wonderful new normal.

Then retreated to my room.

Should've asked my lawyer for full custody of the blanket and mug.

I awoke the next morning and everyone was gone. Prince was in his crate. The tree had been unplugged.

The kitchen was a mess. But my family seemed to be doing okay. Our marriage was quiet. We didn't fight. So the kids didn't see the tension and unrest. Even after the separation, we were

friendly. So maybe, inviting Dad over wasn't awkward to them —
it was just family. Maybe that was one thing Tim and I got right.

CHAPTER 16

I awoke early Christmas morning, and so far, I felt good. *Really* good. Relaxed in a way I don't recall feeling in years. I didn't have to think about getting up, opening gifts, making breakfast. My biggest responsibility at the moment was Prince. Instead of a walk, I decided he could just do his business in the backyard.

I turned on Christmas music and let Prince out. I went to the kitchen and was assaulted again by the mess—including my dog mug, sitting dirty in the sink—a reminder of the Christmas Eve home invasion by my ex. It took no time to clean. Why hadn't they done that before they left? Dishwasher started, counters wiped, and dog mug hand-washed, I made myself a cup of Christmas blend.

Prince came back in—my poor baby was cold—so I tucked him in my chair with my blanket. I set my phone, coffee, and tablet on the side table and snuggled in with my boy.

I felt gratitude and peace. Calm in a way that was foreign to me on Christmas morning. Totally unexpected.

It was too early to call my family, so I opened my NYT app and worked the daily crossword. I sat there for the next hour, leisurely sipping coffee, listening to Christmas music, and playing my games. I could get used to this no-stress Christmas trend. I was loving it.

At 8:30, I knew the Proctor family was waking up. Our family group text started pinging. It included my parents, all my siblings, most of their spouses, and any of the kids old enough to have a cell phone.

The first photo came from my brother and his family on the East Coast: matching pajamas, torn wrapping paper, smiling faces. Same an hour later from my brother in Chicago, and then my sister in California. I picked up Prince, snapped a selfie in front of the tree, and sent it to the group. My smile was genuine. The younger kids loved seeing Prince.

At 9 a.m., I called my parents. I talked to Mom, then Dad, then my brother, then each of the kids jumped on. By the time I ended that call, I needed to start getting ready for the day with Disha.

I quickly texted Aaron and Morgan to say I'd call them that evening—I didn't want to disturb their time with their dad. I texted Amy too. We needed to catch up.

I sent a gif to the running group—a Santa running from reindeer, his pants missing, candy cane boxers on display.

I sent David a separate message. Probably stupid. But a group text didn't feel like enough.

Me: Merry Christmas to you and Simon. Hope you enjoy your day.

He immediately replied:

David: Merry Christmas to you too.

I went and got dressed.

Disha and I had a fun-filled day.

The Gaylord was decked out, and we wandered through the decorations, taking pictures and selfies. The ballroom for brunch was stunning, with soft music and gorgeous tables. We stuffed ourselves and drank champagne.

The ICE! exhibit was remarkable- especially the larger-than-life nativity carved in clear ice. It took my breath away.

We roamed around a bit more until it was time to head to the movies.

The day was easy, uneventful, and exactly what I needed.

I called Morgan first.

"Merry Christmas, sweetheart."

"Merry Christmas, Mom." She said it in the exact same tone she uses when Starbucks is out of oat milk—half tragedy, half personal insult.

This is usually my cue to ask what's wrong. What if I didn't?

"Did you have a nice day?" I asked instead, all casual-like. Santa must have left boundaries in my stocking this year.

"Um, no. I am never doing that again."

This is where I'm supposed to say What? Tell me everything. I said nothing. It was almost... fun.

"Mom, are you there?"

"I'm here, sweetie. I figured you weren't done yet. I was waiting."

"Oh. Well, Dad's house was terrible. You know what happened with New Mexico. But then Dad was all sad and wanted me and Aaron to stay with him. So, okay, we stayed. He said he'd make a big Christmas breakfast. And guess what?"

I was really getting the hang of this non-reacting thing. It's easier than I thought and slightly more entertaining. Morgan didn't let the silence stretch this time.

"When Dad finally got up, he made us oatmeal and toast. Then he went back to his room and stayed on the phone all day. No gifts. No tree. No stocking, no Christmas songs, no church, no cookies. And if that's not bad enough, Aaron ditched me to keep him company. I was stuck there all-day watching TV with Dad. Aaron went to Katie's parents."

I made the appropriate sympathetic noise, even though I was thinking: You're twenty-two, Morgan. You could have maybe helped with breakfast. You could have left. There were options besides whining.

"I'm sorry it wasn't a good day, sweetheart. It sounds like your dad might be going through something. I'm glad you were able to be there with him."

(And maybe that would make her feel just a little guilty. She could be impressively self-centered—gold medal material if it were an Olympic sport.)

"I guess. But next year, I'm making the plans. We'll be at your house on Christmas Eve and Christmas morning. Then we can have lunch or dinner with Dad."

"That sounds fine. But let's see what next year looks like when it's next year. Things change. What if Aaron and Katie get married? He might want to spend time with her family. One day you might get married—or want to go skiing with friends. That's okay. You're adults. You get to decide what you want to do-"

"-but only for yourself," she finished, rolling her eyes audibly.

"Exactly."

"I don't think I like this adult thing."

I let that go. Sympathy wouldn't help. She needed to toughen up. (Being 22 with no tree and a bowl of oatmeal on Christmas isn't exactly in the category of personal trauma.)

"Did you want to hear about my day?"

"I'm sorry, Mom. How was your day?"

(I'm not entirely convinced she wanted to know—still too wrapped up in her own pity parade. I kept it short.)

"I need to make some more calls before it gets too late. I love you, sweetheart. I'll see you next week."

"Bye, Mom. Love you."

Next up on my call list, Aaron.

"Merry Christmas, Mom!" He sounded upbeat, like someone who'd just won a free queso for life.

"Merry Christmas!"

"How was your day?"

This is what I mean about Aaron—he asks. It's a skill. I gave him the quick version of my delightful day, complete with brunch, ice sculptures, and the fact that champagne apparently makes me think I'm a professional photographer.

"I talked to Morgan," I said. I didn't want him to have to rehash it, and I certainly wasn't about to apologize for not whisking her away from her oatmeal apocalypse.

"Yeah? It was a little rough, to be honest."

I could hear the diplomacy in his voice. Translation: It was bad, but I wasn't there to throw Dad under the bus at Christmas. I decided to change the subject.

"Are you still at Katie's?"

"I'm at her parents' place. She's right here."

"Nice. Can I talk to her for a sec?"

"Sure."

"Merry Christmas!" Katie's voice was warm and happy.

"Merry Christmas! Did you have a nice holiday?"

"Yes! Even better now that Aaron's here."

It was the kind of thing that makes a mom's heart do a little happy somersault—though I'm pretty sure somewhere, Morgan just rolled her eyes without knowing why.

"Well, I won't keep you. Just wanted to say Merry Christmas. I'll see you next week."

My last call was to Amy.

"Merry Christmas!"

"Merry Christmas. You doing okay?" she asked, suspicious—like she was braced for me to say I'd spent the day drinking boxed wine and crying into a cheese log.

"I'm great!" I gave her the highlight reel—no mess, no stress, and yes, Santa had apparently decided to leave Tim under my tree last night. She had a few choice words for that, none of them printable in a church bulletin.

Then I told her about dinner at Amigos Cocina and the gifts. I could practically hear her eyebrows go up when I mentioned the bracelet.

"Yours had a heart on it?" she asked.

"Yes. Little silver beads, crystal heart charm."

"And Disha's had... what? Pentagon? Octagon? Something without an actual pulse?"

"Yes. Very pretty. Why?"

"A heart, Renee?"

"Amy, come on. We've been over this."

"We have. And I still think you're wrong. Have you considered just walking up and planting one on him?"

I'd considered it. I'd also considered that it would likely be followed by me having to move to a new city under an assumed name.

"No, Amy. Friends don't do that. And besides, I like living here under my actual name."

"You're hopeless."

"I prefer the term 'strategically cautious.'"

"Fine. But when he shows up dating someone else, I'm sending you a sympathy plant. And I'll pick something hard to kill so you'll have to look at it for years and think of this moment."

"Wow. Nothing says 'I love you' like a cactus of regret."

She laughed. We moved on to complaining about our sister Ellie, which was safer territory for both of us.

I sat on my sofa-Prince asleep on my lap, a soft glow from tree lights, and a fire in the fireplace. I took a moment to reflect on my holiday.

I think the most important gift I got this year was peace—a kind of peace I knew would stay with me for a very long time.

CHAPTER 17

It was New Year's Eve. Amy and I had big plans to stay at her house, eat pizza and leftover Christmas cookies, and play cards. Mattie was staying at a friend's house. I was a little surprised that she didn't have other plans. We didn't hang out much on weekends when I was married. I assumed she went out more- with friends or dates, or boyfriends. My sister was gorgeous, smart, and fun- the whole package. I always imagined she had to hand out raffle tickets to keep the line of men in order. Turns out, her weekends were less nightclub and more Netflix. I had never known her to have a serious boyfriend. For someone who was eager to see me get out there, she was one to talk.

I brought my pajamas and Prince. I was going to stay the night. Neither of us liked to be on the roads on new year's- too many drunks. After Amy's husband was killed by a drunk driver, sober driving became more than a rule for our family—it became a responsibility to which we all firmly committed.

We had gotten comfortable and pizza was on its way. We were on our second round of hand and foot. She was, as usual, kicking my butt already. We got on the topic of new year's resolutions.

"Honestly, I don't see the point." she said, as she scored another 300 points. "No one keeps their new year's resolution, so why bother."

"I noticed that when I had a gym membership. The first two weeks in January, the gym was busy like a close out sale at DSW. By week three, it was just a couple of guys grunting in the free weights." I discarded, ending my turn.

Amy drew a card, "When did you have a gym membership?"

"I had one a few years ago. I wanted to lose a few pounds after Christmas. I only went a few weeks. It was way too crowded."

We laughed.

I hadn't made a New Year's resolution in years. But as Amy counted out her cards, I realized that underneath the peace I had found, there was still a question. I didn't want another Liam, and David was clearly in the "just friends" column. But somewhere between the cookies and Amy's relentless winning streak, I started to wonder what else might be out there for me.

A test. An experiment. A toe in the water.

Was it even possible- for *me*?

"Well, don't fall out of your chair, but I want to try that 'go on a lot of first dates' thing." I said, as I discarded.

Amy stopped and stared in disbelief. "What did you say?"

"You heard me. I think I need to get out there and see what I want or even if I want." I also just had a brilliant idea- I would make Amy do it, too.

"Wow! Good for you." She closed another clean book.

"I have no idea what to do next." I took my turn.

"Let's finish this round, and I'll show you."

Amy drew one more time, and went out again. There was no way I would catch up.

Amy had grabbed her tablet and we sat side by side on the couch. Prince jumped up and fell asleep in my lap.

"There are basically three good ways to meet someone: Friends of friends, church, or online. Tonight, we will focus on online."

"OK. You mean like *Flame Up*?"

"Lord no! That's just for hook ups."

"Hook ups?"

"Yeah, people who just want to have sex." Nope. Not me. I was open to *dating*. I will cross the sex bridge later.

"Then which one should I try?" There were a couple of different ones, but we decided on the one that used advanced AI to match you with prospective partners. There was a monthly fee- and it cost about what a gym membership would, the going rate for a good new year's resolution. Amy assured me that it wasn't as likely to be just for hook ups, and was worth the money.

I got signed up, but not before I convinced Amy to join me. Mission accomplished. It took a lot of cajoling, minor guilt-tripping, and one threat to hide the remaining Christmas cookies, but I wore her down.

Amy started my profile first.

"Age?" I told her.

"Height?" I told her. "Should I round up? I mean, I've worn heels before."

"No. If you round up, you'll spend the first ten minutes of every date defending your shoes."

"Do you want kids?" I gave her a look. "At this point? I'd rather adopt a succulent."

"Drinking habits."

"Yes, socially."

Amy snorted. "Should we clarify what 'socially' means in your case? Like... 'is there vodka in that?'"

"Hobbies & Interests"

"Running, reading, live music, trying new restaurants, dogs."

She typed: "Running, live music, food adventures, dog lover."

"What happened to reading?" I asked.

"Nobody swipes right for 'reading.' It says 'I'm introverted and will glare at you if you dog-ear my paperback.'"

"Morning person or night owl?"

"Neither. I'm more of a 'functional from 9 to 9, but only with coffee' person."

"Going with night owl-it's sexier. Favorite pizza topping?"

"Is that really a thing people match on?"

"Apparently. It says it's a 'core compatibility factor.'"

"Put olives. Anyone who doesn't like olives probably wouldn't like me. I can be a little salty."

"My ideal Saturday"

"Coffee, crossword, walk with Prince, maybe a nap, shoe sale."

Amy groaned. "That's a brochure for an assisted living community. How about 'exploring new places with good company'?"

Then came the "quirky" prompts.

Two truths and a lie: I rattled them off. "I once ran a 5K in a Halloween costume, I've been skydiving, and I've never eaten sushi."

"Which is the lie?" Amy asked.

"Skydiving. Obviously. I'm not jumping out of a perfectly good plane unless it's on fire."

We moved to photos, which turned into a heated debate about lighting, angles, and whether Prince should appear.

"He's cuter than I am. He'll get all the swipes," I argued.

"Exactly. We're selling you, not him. No free dog bait."

Amy had dozens of options—every one of them perfect. Sun-kissed on a beach. Laughing in a café. Looking effortlessly stunning in a candid shot at a wedding. She looked at ease, carefree, like she'd been followed around by a personal photographer who caught her in her most flattering light.

I, on the other hand, had about six recent photos, most of which looked like I was either mid-sneeze or silently wondering if I'd locked my car. In half of them, my hair was doing something weird, and in the others, I looked like I had mild gas.

After two hours, three minor arguments, and one bowl of popcorn later, we finally uploaded our profiles. We each downloaded the mobile app and declared ourselves done. Ready for a match—or whatever the algorithm thought was a match.

Well, *almost* done. Given that we were both on the same platform, and of the same age, it was possible that she and I might get paired with the same person. We made a pact—if we got matched with the same guy, we'd talk before messaging. No one needed a Lifetime Original movie about sisters falling out over "Greg, 54, enjoys grilling and stamp collecting."

The site promised matches by tomorrow, so we resumed our card game.

I felt like someone's old sofa for sale on Craigslist—gently used, decent condition, a few emotional stains, but still structurally sound. And now, officially "on the market."

I'd done it. I was proud of myself for following through. Also terrified. Also, a little nauseous.

Was I really ready? Probably not. But I was also curious—curious enough to try.

And maybe, just maybe, part of me hoped the distraction would quiet the part of me that still lit up when David walked into a room.

Happy New Year to me.

We resumed our card game, struggling to stay awake until midnight. When the clock struck twelve, our phones lit up with texts from friends and family. We sat at the table, replying between yawns and bites of leftover cookies.

Among the messages was one from David, sent to both Disha and me.

Happy New Year! Hope you two are staying out of trouble.

It was warm. Friendly. Just enough.

It also felt like a very clear signal—things were back to normal. We were back to normal. Just friends.

That made my decision to try dating a little easier.

And I was still a little disappointed.

Not enough to say it out loud. Not even to Amy. But enough to feel it.

The following morning, Amy and I had coffee, and we sat on the couch eager to see what matches we got.

I had 5. I reviewed the profiles, and there was no way that these guys were compatible. There must be something wrong with the AI. Or maybe it wasn't "artificial intelligence" at all—more like "artificial stupidity," programmed by someone's Uncle Gary who thinks women my age should be grateful for a man with all his own teeth.

Is this it? Is this the best I had to hope for?

If so, I might as well take up knitting and mahjong now—at least then I'd have something to do while my "match" napped in front of the game.

I was hoping to meet someone kind, who liked kids and dogs, maybe even a runner. Someone who laughed easily. Liked to dance. You know- basic stuff. Not "owns five grills and naps through football season" stuff.

I looked over at Amy. She was completely unaffected, and just kept swiping left.

"What?" she asked.

"I don't think I can do this Amy, this is so bad."

"Renee, it's OK. I know it can be a shock at first, but it's a numbers game. If you are not interested, swipe left. There will be more. Trust me."

I gave it a go, and I had swiped left on all of my matches.

I decided that I couldn't let this decision disrupt the peace I had found over the holiday. I closed the dating app, opened my NYT app, and did my puzzles.

I would try again some other day.

CHAPTER 18

It was the second week in January. Run club resumed tonight, and I was so glad. I was ready to get back into a comfortable routine. Unfortunately, the weather wasn't ready- it was extremely cold, and threatening an ice storm later in the evening. It was the kind of cold that I wouldn't run in. But I really was ready to get out and see my friends, so I went to Moonwinks in time for any runners to return.

I headed up to our usual table on the third floor. Moonwinks had covered the patio with plastic and turned on the heaters- it was surprisingly pleasant. I sat alone, remembering my first time here just a few months ago. It was incredible how much of my life had changed since then. Not just my dress size- running definitely helped me manage my weight better. But how something like joining a run club led to forming meaningful friendships, reaching personal goals, and finding a feeling of contentment. It brought me out of the house, out of my head, and into something fulfilling.

Scott and Ashley came in first. We said hello and hugged and they set off for the bar for beers. Lonnie was next, followed by David, then Disha- all of them red faced, noses running. They looked nearly frozen. The rest of the club must have stayed home- and I couldn't blame them.

I was so relieved at the normalcy of this time with my friends. We all laughed, and shared stories from our holiday. But conversation quickly moved on to what was next. I think that is the nature of runners-they look at the road ahead, not behind.

Next up, The Cowtown. The Cowtown races were held at the end of February every year. The race starts and ends in Fort Worth's cultural district at Will Rogers, runs through the historic Stockyards, through downtown and circles TCU and Fort Worth's southside. They have a 5K, 10K, half marathon, Marathon and an Ultra Marathon.

Everyone at the table but me and Disha were planning to run one of the races. Ashley, Scott and Lonnie were planning to run the marathon on Sunday. David was running the half on Saturday- and he said Pete was as well. Since neither Disha nor I were planning to run, we decided to be in charge of the cheering section. We talked about special tech shirts for the run club to wear-well, Disha mentioned it. I agreed to help her find sponsors.

Everything was just really normal. Until it wasn't.

Everyone else had left, and it was just me, Disha and David.

"Hey, did you guys see that new movie comes out this weekend?" I asked. It was a new movie from Marvel studios. It looked really good- action-packed. We had all talked about it once before, and I knew they also were interested in seeing it.

"Want to go Friday night?" I asked.

"I'm in." said Disha.

"I can't," said David. And I got a vibe. Not the vague, could-be-anything kind- this was sharp, certain. I knew what was coming before he even said it. I held my breath.

I felt the drop before it happened—like that split second on a roller coaster when you know the bottom is about to fall out. My heart was already muttering, "No, no, no..."

Maybe it was just a friend. A work colleague. Maybe-

"Hot date?" Disha teased.

He looked right at me, and in that split second, I saw it- the quiet confirmation of what I already knew.

"Something like that." He looked away, towards Disha. "I'm meeting someone for drinks."

I was right. I felt the weight of his words pressing on my chest, threatening to squeeze the air from my lungs, and tears from my eyes.

"What about Saturday?" He asked.

I knew I couldn't let him see it. Couldn't let even a flicker cross my face.

I couldn't let anyone see how broken I felt.

I was his friend- truly- and that meant swallowing the lump in my throat and keeping the rest to myself. All the sadness, regret, and sharp little shards of disappointment

"I can't Saturday- I have plans to go to dinner with Amy." It was a lie. I just didn't think I could go to the movies with him, share popcorn. It felt too intimate all of a sudden- even if Disha would be there.

Any time I was with David, I felt something intimate. I always had- even that first time I met him- at the court house. I felt the slightest connection even then.

"You guys go on without me." He offered. "I need to take Simon to see it."

I got the sense that he was avoiding being too close to me too. Though I wasn't sure why.

Disha and I made plans and we all headed out.

Alone in my car, I hung my head.

I knew this day would come- had felt it out there, circling like a storm waiting to make landfall.

Knowing didn't soften the blow.

It still knocked the wind out of me- left me feeling empty.

I hadn't missed my chance with David- I'd given it away, smothered under the weight of my own fear.

And I was disappointed in myself for that.

For every moment I'd let pass without saying what I really wanted.

How many times was I going to let fear run my life?

How many regrets could one person carry before they crushed her?

And then another thought came, sharp and mean: why did it feel like he was the one nursing a bruise?

He had his chance too- and he'd walked right past it.

Of course he had. Because he never wanted me like that.

He's just a nice guy with good manners. A good friend. I was a fool for thinking any different.

And I was an idiot for thinking it might be anything more.

All those "connections" I swore I felt?

Just me, grasping at straws.

It was all bullshit.

Later that evening, I sat in my living room, the only light coming from the fireplace. Prince slept in my lap, and I absently stroked his fur, taking comfort in his warmth and the steady rise and fall of his breathing.

The ache in my chest had dulled to a low hum. I felt steadier now.

Heartbreak can make you run- or make you fight. Most people run. I'd been running for a long time.

But when you touch something warm- when it's gone, you chase that feeling.

David reminded me that what I wanted was possible. That it was still out there. Maybe I could find it with someone else.

I felt a resolve- a purpose.

A voice in my head was clear, steady: *Don't let another chance pass you by. You won't always get it right. You won't always win. But you have to try.*

Playing it safe had kept me comfortable.

Trying was the only thing that might make me happy.

I opened the dating app.

Maybe it wouldn't be David.

But maybe—just maybe—there was someone else out there for me.

CHAPTER 19

Over the next few days, I'd come back from walking Prince and browse the dating app for potentially viable dating options- what I'd dubbed *PVs*. The term caught on with Amy. She started calling them PVs too.

Unfortunately, it was slim pickings out there. So far, neither of us had found any PVs.

We'd also created a short list of minimum requirements for consideration:

- If one or more photos showed him with a bare chest- or any other bare parts- **swipe left**.
- If a woman had clearly been cropped out of a picture- **swipe left**. Come on, dude, make a little effort and take your own photo.
- If there was a toilet or urinal in the background- **hard swipe left**. We even saw one where a guy was *at* the urinal in the background. Gross.
- If his status said "separated"- **swipe left**. We agreed to be open only once that changed to *divorced*.
- If he'd had more than two prior marriages- **swipe left**. Shout-out to the guy who'd been married *five times*- keep dreaming, friend.

I had a feeling the list would grow with time, but this was our starting point. A girl has to have some standards.

We'd both received quite a few messages- Amy more than me, but who's counting? At first, I tried to respond to every single one. It got overwhelming fast. Amy assured me it was perfectly acceptable to ignore messages if I wasn't interested. That freed up a lot of my time. Still, I felt a tiny pang of guilt whenever I deleted one without replying. It just felt... impolite.

So far, no one had reached out that I genuinely wanted to talk to.

"What do you think about this one?" Amy asked, holding out her phone. "Michael S."

"For me or for you?"

"For you! He's not my type," she said.

"Why not?"

"I don't know. I think his eyes are too close together." Oh, great—so *beady-eyed* was okay for me, just not her type?

"Swipe left," I said flatly. We returned to our scrolling.

"I have one for *you*," I said, holding out my screen. Amy looked briefly, then went back to hers.

"No."

"Why not? He's cute, has a decent job, and kids around Mattie's age."

"I already looked at him. I don't remember why I said no, but... no."

And so it went. We were swiping left like we were directing traffic in a turn lane.

Then a new message came in.

"Hey, check this guy out. I just got a message from him." I shifted closer to Amy and pulled up the profile.

His name was Milo N.

According to his profile, Milo was my age. Divorced. Grown kids. Decent job.

He was 5'11". He was a *runner*- excellent. I still hadn't swiped left.

He liked live music. Played the piano- nice. Still not swiping.

Enjoyed dancing. Read books in his spare time (apparently, that *was* perfectly fine to put in your profile after all.)

I was officially intrigued.

His main photo was a simple headshot. He had a kind smile and crinkles at the corners of his eyes, like someone who smiled often.

"Let's see the rest of his photos," Amy said.

I pulled them up. They were all casual- jeans, running clothes, shorts, a ball cap. He looked like an athletic man of average height with a nice, open face. No bare torsos, no cropped-out exes, no bathroom plumbing in sight.

No violations. No red flags.

I was nervous.

"I'm doing it, Amy."

"This is exciting," she said, leaning in as I opened the message.

MiloN-McKinney: *Hello Renee.*

I noticed your profile—your beautiful eyes first. Then how much we had in common.
I'm a runner too, and I love dogs. I have a schnauzer named Mickey.
I was hoping we could meet for a drink or coffee. It would be a privilege to get to know you better.
I hope to hear from you. But in any case, all the best. —Milo

"What do you think?" I asked.

"I think you should go for it. What've you got to lose?"

She was right. *No regrets*, right?

I began typing:

ReneeM-Den: *Hi Milo.*

Thank you for your message and your kind words.
Let's do it!

Nope. Backspace, backspace, backspace.

I'd love to meet up.

Much better.

I hit send.

◆ ◆ ◆

The Date

Milo and I arranged to meet halfway between where we each lived. We agreed on 6 p.m. Tuesday. I had forgotten how terrible Metroplex traffic was at that time and was barely on time. My nerves were completely frayed when I pulled into the parking lot.

Milo had suggested we meet at a nice steakhouse bar, so I dressed a little nicer—black slacks, a sweater, and heels. I was even wearing earrings. I reserved earrings for when I really wanted to elevate my look a notch.

I walked into the bar. It was dimly lit but about half full of happy hour patrons- definitely the two-fingers-of-bourbon executive crowd. I spotted who had to be Milo at a high two-top near the bar. He saw me, smiled, and stood as we made eye contact.

I wasn't sure what I was seeing.

He looked like Milo's photos- if you ran them through one of those "age yourself" filters and kept going until the app begged you to stop. For a man supposedly in his late 40s, he looked not a day younger than late 60s. He *was* a handsome man. But his neck, his hands, the way he slightly stooped- he seemed so much older. He was even wearing Old Spice cologne—a scent I recognized because it had been my father's favorite.

The second thing I noticed as we talked: his face didn't move. Not at all. His eyebrows, forehead, maybe even his *nose*- frozen. His eyes never got larger or smaller. He couldn't squint. It was like he was perpetually surprised. He spoke, but barely moved his mouth. It was like talking to a wax figure who could order wine.

The waiter came by. Milo knew him by name, and they were very friendly. We each ordered a glass of wine, though I wondered if Milo might need a straw to drink his. I also wondered if they might bring him a bib-in case the straw failed.

Despite the surprise of his appearance, Milo was a genuinely nice man- refined, polite, and easy to talk to. We discovered we had plenty in common, and the conversation never dragged. I couldn't say I didn't enjoy myself.

A man not much younger than me approached our table. He was dressed in a suit and tie.

"Hey, Pop," he said to Milo.

Milo stood and hugged him.

Poor kid. He got his father's genetics, because there was *no way* this 48-year-old man had a son his age.

Milo introduced him. His son, James, was the manager of the steakhouse. I wondered how many of Milo's dates poor James had to meet. They chatted for a bit.

"It was nice to meet you, Renee," James said before heading off.

Milo leaned toward me like he wanted to share a secret. "Would you believe I'm not really 48?"

Sure, Milo. And I'm 29

"NO?" I said, faking disbelief. "How old are you?"

"I'm actually 68. But my doctor insists I have the body and metabolism of a 48-year-old. And I'm much more active than most people my age."

And there it was.

We finished our wine, and Milo walked out with me. He wasn't quite in the "peak physical condition" his doctor claimed— unless peak condition meant strolling at the speed of a museum tour.

"Thank you, Milo. It was really nice to meet you."

"Would you like to go out again sometime?" he asked.

Milo was such a nice guy. I hated to hurt his feelings. But I'd rather slather myself in honey and sit on an ant hill buck naked than do this again.

"Milo, you're a very nice man. I just don't feel any spark here. I hope we can part as friends," I said.

He smiled- I think. "Of course, dear. I'll walk you to your car."

Milo walked me to my car and wished me a good night.

I was in a state of total disbelief.

I got on the freeway toward home.

"Hey Siri, call Amy."

"Calling favorite sister." I don't know how she did it, but that's what happens when any of us use voice command to call.

"Hey! So how was it?"

"You are never going to believe this."

CHAPTER 20

The next day, the weather was extremely pleasant, sunny and had reached the low 70's. It was a great day to run. The weather inspired me to conquer both the miles and the awkwardness I was feeling about David.

I timed my arrival so I could take off running the second I got there. Quick hello, and I was gone. As always, David circled back for me. We ran in easy silence at first, then slipped into conversation- kids, work, the dog. But not dating. Friends talked about that kind of thing, sure. But this wasn't a normal friendship, and I wasn't ready to hear about some woman laughing at his jokes. I liked pretending those laughs were mine. By the time we reached Moonwinks, it almost felt like before. Almost. From now on, I'd always look at him a little differently.

I didn't stay as late as I usually did- just one quick beer. Disha and I had made plans to work on sponsors for the Cowtown race shirts after yoga Saturday, and I took off.

The following week at run club, We were about a half mile in when a blur of fur shot across my path. One second I was upright, the next I was kissing asphalt.

"Renee!" David was there before I could even swear properly.

From behind us, Pete yelled, "Man down! Somebody call Animal Control!"

"I'm fine," I mumbled into the pavement. I was not fine. My knees burned, my head hurt, and I could taste blood. My eyes were watering from the intense pain. I never looked great at the end of a run — today was just going to be a more dramatic version.

"You're bleeding."

"Adds character."

He helped me up, his arm sliding firmly around my waist, his shoulder steady under mine, his warmth wrapping around me like a blanket. He matched his steps to my uneven limp, eyes never leaving me, as if getting me back to Moonwinks was the only thing in the world that mattered.

"You're shaking. I think you're in shock."

"I'll be fine."

"ER," he said.

"I don't need—"

"ER." Leaving no room for argument.

And here's the weird part — I didn't argue. I let him take me. I just let him steer me toward his car like there was a lollipop waiting if I didn't make a fuss.

At the ER, I was sprawled on an exam table while David sat in a chair beside me. I felt bad he'd had to bring me here. In hindsight, I could've called Amy. But David was there, and I was glad.

"Thanks for this," I said, ice packs on my knees and face. "Sorry you had to play chauffeur."

"Of course. I'm sorry you got hurt, but I wouldn't be anywhere else."

The doctor came in. "Renee, I'm Dr. Venkatesh. That was quite a fall."

"Yeah — no one taught those dogs about personal space," I

quipped.

"You have a slight concussion, some scratches, and you'll have bruising tomorrow. You can go home, but no driving for 48 hours."

When the doctor left, David pulled the blanket around me a little tighter. He didn't have to be here, but he was. And for that, I was grateful.

Once I was discharged, we left. David drove me home, but offered to help me get my car in a couple of days when I was cleared to drive. He had also texted Amy earlier, and she was waiting at my house when we arrived. He helped me into the house, and once he was sure I was settled, he left.

I had changed into pajamas and Amy was helping me climb into bed.

"That man has it so bad for you."

If only that were true.

CHAPTER 21

After a couple days of rest and the all-clear from my doctor that my brain was still intact, I slid back into a routine that felt both comfortable and familiar- run club every week, skipping only when the cold made my bones ache and my common sense kicked in. David and I had resumed our easy rhythm. It was good- a relief. Like taking off a bra you've been wearing since 7 a.m. and finally breathing properly again.

Disha and I locked in five sponsors for the Cowtown race shirts, got the artwork approved, and placed the order. Project done, gold star for us.

I still peeked at the dating app now and then, but it was mostly just me swiping left like I was fanning away a bad smell- *Prince was that you?* Hard to trust after Milo-gate.

Three weeks later, I was driving home from run club when my phone lit up with a call from Mary, a friend from church. Mary and I met two years ago serving on the Easter committee. She was lovely, my parents' age, and the type of woman who could make "Would you like to chair the bake sale?" sound like an honor and not a death sentence.

We did the usual small talk before she got to it. "Renee, you remember my son, Stewart?"

"Of course, Mary." I did. Stewart was maybe a couple of years older than me, and the last time I'd seen him he was married with a couple of kids.

"Well, Renee, Stewart got divorced last year. I was talking to him the other day and mentioned that you also were divorced. He asked if he could have your number. Would that be OK?"

Oh man. When your Catholic friend who's your mom's age asks for a favor, no good Catholic girl can say no. It's basically in the catechism.

I didn't recall much about Stewart—he wasn't drop-dead gorgeous, but he wasn't a swamp troll either. From memory: about 5'10", a little on the softer side, nice enough demeanor. Plus, Mary was a sweetheart.

Amy had always said dating through friends or church was a solid plan. Mary was both. "Sure, Mary. That would be fine."

Mary wasted no time sending Stewart my number, and he wasted no time calling me. He asked if we could meet for a drink and talk. Get to know each other. I agreed. Because of Mary. And I'm catholic, and I didn't want to go to hell for not having a drink with Stewart. It was one drink. How bad could it be?

I met Stewart on Friday at a bar in town. It was on the top floor of a two-story building that faced west. Large panoramic windows allowed patrons to sip wine and watch the sunset over the power lines and warehouses. It was pure magic.

Stewart was already there when I arrived. I walked to where he was sitting half way through a cocktail. He stood and hugged me hello. I don't recall ever having hugged Stewart in the past. I'd only ever met him in passing at church. You know- *This is my son Stewart. Nice to meet you Stewart, You too.* That's it. But I guess we have moved on to hugging.

I ordered a glass of wine, and Stewart ordered another cocktail.

Stewart and I chatted, it was comfortable enough, but I wouldn't have even said we chatted like old friends. We caught up on the kids, how our parents were doing, we talked a little about our jobs. Wine drained, I started to say my goodbyes.

"I was hoping we could run across the street and grab some tacos. Come on, it's Friday night. What else have you got to do?"

Ugh. I could think of a million things I could be doing that would be preferential to more time with Stewart- clean the garage, pick lint off my sofa, scoop dog poop. But I felt like I couldn't say "no"- not to my catholic friend's son. If she heard I declined dinner, it might get back to Father Weston, or God. I had no clue how many Hail Mary's I would have to say to atone for that.

Catholic guilt wins again. "OK."

We headed down to street level to make the short walk to the taco place. We grabbed a table, and Stewart ordered a margarita. I just had ice water. The waiter brought our chips and salsa.

Having said most of what I could think to say to Stewart at the wine bar, the conversation got more awkward. There were long moments of silence.

The waiter came again, not fast enough though, and we each ordered our meals. Stewart ordered another margarita. Ugh. He was already showing signs of a man who was overserved. For Mary, and my personal commitment to sober driving, I knew I had to stay with him until he was sober enough to drive. I hoped it wouldn't take long. But friends don't let friends drink and drive. I would still not have called Stewart a friend, but Mary was.

I flagged the waiter down and asked him to bring us both some ice water. It did little good. Stewart didn't drink it.

The food arrived faster than expected. Somehow, Stewart's margarita glass was empty again and the waiter dropped a new one in front of him. I didn't even see when he asked for it. He was throwing back margaritas like they were M&M's.

I excused myself, and left the table. I flagged down the waiter and threatened him with his life if he brought one more margarita to our table.

I was walking back to my table in time to see Stewart sliding off his chair towards the floor. I caught him just in time. I got him back in his chair, and I convinced him to drink some water.

He was upright, sipping water, and was half awake. At least he wasn't causing a scene. I sat in my chair then, and flagged the waiter.

"May I have the check, please."

The waiter brought the check. Stewart looked at it briefly, struggling to focus. I think he tried moving his arm to take it, but it was just flailing around aimlessly. I grabbed the check, groaned, and threw my credit card on it. Apparently, atonement wasn't cheap.

The waiter came back by, and I gave it to him.

"Hey Stewart, where are your keys buddy?" I was going to have to drive him home.

"I can drive." He insisted. He could have said "RIde or die" or "Try and Lie," I wasn't sure. He was barely coherent.

"I'll drive you buddy- give me your keys." I was using the same tone with Stewart that I used when I was potty training the kids. And Prince. "Boom boom like a good boy."

"No! You no dirimmehom." He slurred.

The waiter returned, I signed the credit card slip, and grabbed my card. I stood up, and put on my coat.

"Stewart, I am telling you right now, hand me your keys." He was in trouble now. I used my mom tone. The "just try me" one, followed by the mom death stare. Brought out the big guns.

"No!"

"Stewart, the only way you are leaving this restaurant is with me holding your keys, or in hand cuffs. Which will it be?" I was done screwing around.

He handed me his keys.

"Let's go". I helped him put on his coat, and I grabbed his arm to help him outside. We were outside walking towards his car, when he abruptly stopped. I assumed he needed to vomit or something. He turned to me, and before I could say anything, his mouth was on mine, and his tongue was down my throat.

When I got over the absolute shock, I pushed him off.

"What the hell, Stewart!?" This would haunt me for the rest of my life. Drunk taco kisses. Gross!

"I wan do all nigh" He slurred.

"No Stewart. You don't do that ever, to anyone. It's assault. I am starting to think you want to be in handcuffs."

"Wiff you?" And he laughed drunkenly.

"Let's go."

I grabbed his arm roughly, and dragged him down the street. We managed to make it to his car without further incident. I got him in the passenger side, then got in the driver side. He was driving some foreign car, and I couldn't figure out how to start it.

"Stewart, how do I start your car?"

He turned his head, and refused to answer me.

"So, help me Stewart, you tell me right this second, or I am calling your Mother. I have had enough!"

Stewart pushed a button and his car started.

I knew generally where Stewart lived, and headed that way.

When we reached the point where I needed directions, I looked over to find Stewart passed out.

Great. I pulled into QuikTrip.

I shook him. "Stewart, wake up. Stewart." Nothing.

I could call his Mom, but it was really late. I really didn't want to worry her. I am sure Stewart had worried her quite enough. I'd only do that as a last resort.

I checked the glove box for any papers that might have his address on it. Nothing.

I had one more idea, but it was going to be really unpleasant. I got out of the car. I walked over to the passenger side and opened the door. I knew men usually carried their wallets in their back pockets-like the ones that Stewart was sitting on. I had to do this, for Mary. I really didn't want to go to Hell for going out with a drunkard, and not seeing him safely home. I reached my hand in Stewart's back pocket. I cringed at the thought that it was the weight of his ass on my hand. The right pocket was empty. This is where it got risky. I had to lean over him to reach his other pocket. I was afraid of what Stewart would do if he woke up and found me stretched across his lap, grabbing his ass, especially after he swabbed my tonsils with his tongue. This nightmare couldn't get any worse. I did a quick sign of the cross, as I silently pleaded with the man upstairs (or woman) to keep Stewart asleep. I bravely went in. I leaned over, reached into his pocket and hit pay dirt. I pulled his wallet out and opened it-to find two condoms. At this point, I was starting to feel a headache snaking up my neck.

I found his license, plugged the address into my phone, and we were on our way.

We arrived at Stewart's house. I used the garage door opener to get us inside. I was able to get Stewart awake enough to mostly walk into the house. He walked straight back to what I assumed was his bedroom. I was hopeful he was facedown on his bed unconscious.

I sat down on the couch, and ordered my Uber. I would Uber back to my car, and drive home, and forget this night ever happened. I looked up to see Stewart standing there-swaying, in nothing but his Superman boxers and socks.

"You wann shtay?"

I got up, and walked out.

I was standing on the sidewalk waiting for my Uber, when it started to rain.

Just my luck.

My Uber showed up ten minutes later.

I didn't call Amy on my way home to tell her about the fiasco of my evening.

When I spoke with her the next day, I just told her we had drinks and tacos, and no, I wouldn't go out with him again. I thought it might upset her to know the details. It upset me.

I was starting to seriously wonder- *this is what's out there?*

I got a text from Stewart the next day also.

Stewart: *About last night, I think we both agree that we're just not right for one another. There's no reason to continue to see each other.*

No apology. No "thanks for getting my drunk ass home". No accountability.

Not even the threat of a hundred Hail Mary's was enough for me to give him another minute of my time.

I blocked his number.

CHAPTER 22

The big weekend of the Cowtown races had arrived. Disha had arranged a dinner on Friday night at a local Italian restaurant. She explained that long distance runners needed to eat a lot of carbs the night before a race. She really was a genius. First, she arranged for a private room and a pasta buffet with the restaurant at a discount in exchange for a spot on the shirt. Then she was able to promote the dinner on the Cowtown social media pages. She'd created graphics, and even had a website for people to buy tickets. She paid for the event and the shirts with cash to spare, which was donated to the children's hospital in Fort Worth.

David and I checked tickets at the door, slipping back into the familiar groove we'd always seemed to find. Working together had always been like that - shoulder to shoulder, quick smiles, inside jokes no one else heard. It felt...normal.

It was a very early night- runners didn't drink before a big race- after was another story. I knew firsthand how good a cold beer tasted after a run. Disha and I confirmed our plans for the morning, and we all left.

Today was the half marathon. David, Pete, and three others from our group were running.

As planned, Disha swung by at 5:45 a.m. It was freezing- so cold that the sensible part of my brain was halfway back under the covers- but the forecast promised blue skies and 70's later, so I layered up, including the special "Cheering Section" hoodie Disha had made.

Our first stop was Will Rogers, where we'd watch our runners launch into glory. Then we'd leapfrog along the route like caffeinated soccer moms, popping up at different points to yell ourselves hoarse, before meeting them at the finish line.

I brought the essentials: bananas, chocolate milk, and Gatorade —because nothing says "I support you" like handing someone sweaty a bottle of electrolytes.

The starting line buzzed with this electric mix of nerves and grit. You could see it in their faces- eyes locked forward, minds already running the miles ahead. I couldn't help thinking... if we approached life with that kind of intentionality, we'd all probably have better abs and fewer regrets.

The gun went off. Pete came by first, grinning like he'd just been told they were handing out margaritas at mile three. Our Plucky Pete. David followed close behind, eyes on the road, determination carved into his face. I silently sent him a wish for the perfect race- strong legs, steady breath, and maybe something to smile about at mile 12.

We chased them across the city, cheering at stop after stop until we made it back to Will Rogers just in time for the fastest runners to cross. Two of our crew came in first—high fives all around. Pete showed up next, still grinning, barely winded. Honestly, I'm not convinced he even sweats.

And then came David. I snapped a photo right as his foot crossed the finish—face flushed, muscles taut, sunlight catching in a thin sheen of sweat. For one absurd second, I considered sending it to *Sports Illustrated*. He was beautiful.

When David crossed the finish line, sweaty and triumphant, his eyes scanned the crowd until they landed on me. He didn't hesitate - he came straight over, grinning, pulling me into a hug that nearly knocked the air out of my lungs. For a moment, I forgot the noise, the crowd, everything but the solid weight of him and the way it felt like we were celebrating together. Then, he let go, moved down the line to hug the others, and waited with us for the rest of our group to finish.

Sunday was a repeat of Saturday- only longer. While our runners were out racking up miles, Disha and I racked up calories with pan dulce and coffee at Esperanza's on Main, because cheering burns, oh, *at least* seven calories an hour.

There were three in our group today- Lonnie, Ashley, and Scott. Scott came through first, waved, and kept moving. I was surprised; I thought he'd wait for Ashley. Apparently, he had other plans- or maybe he just wanted first dibs on the snack table.

Ten minutes later, Lonnie appeared, collected his high fives, and was gone, like a man late for a meeting.

A minute after that, Ashley rounded the final stretch. Just past the finish line, I spotted someone step into the lane. It was Scott- holding a bouquet of flowers. Disha and I edged closer, because this clearly wasn't about electrolytes.

Ashley crossed, finally spotting him, and her face lit up- pure surprise and delight. Scott kissed her quickly, handed her the bouquet, then dropped to one knee. A photographer appeared like they'd been crouching in the bushes for hours, waiting for this exact moment. The ring box was open.

We couldn't hear the words, but we didn't need to. Ashley said "yes." The crowd erupted. He slid the ring on her finger, they kissed, hugged, and Ashley cried- promptly setting off a chain reaction in at least half a dozen strangers.

I was so happy for them both. Love was beautiful. And in that moment, contagious- and slightly hazardous to mascara.

CHAPTER 23

A week after Cowtown, the Bradford pears bloomed like confetti —and so did the pollen count. Texas spring: gorgeous, lethal to sinuses. Nights still flirted with freezing but never quite got there; days stretched warmer and longer. I was back to morning runs and run club- at least until the spring rains arrived.

Spring is conference season, so I did three short trips over six weeks. Fun and exhausting in equal measure- great dinners and face time, followed by days so people-y my social battery wheezed.

Prince took to Dog Farm Boarding like a champ- clean, spacious indoor pens, acres to run, and daily texted photos with his "report." I knew he was in good hands.

In early April, Scott and Ashley's invitation arrived- June third weekend, "Renee Masters and Guest." I couldn't help thinking of my Christmas dinner plus-one... and whether his said "David Durand and Guest." I put it aside for now. No use walking that road again.

I had just gotten home from having Mother's Day brunch with Aaron, Katie and Morgan. Katie's parents joined us also. It was very nice to meet them. This was a sure sign that Aaron was very serious about Katie. I was very happy for them both. She was a very sweet girl, and seemed to adore him as much as he adored her. They had built their relationship based on a deep respect for one another and a true friendship.

I was sitting in my back yard, watching Prince, now almost 30 pounds, run around the yard. I was on my tablet playing on my NYT app and enjoying a beautiful day.

Out of curiosity I checked Date4U. Twenty messages had piled up. Most were easy left-swipes- until one made me pause.

Michael M. was two years older than me. Divorced once. Two grown children. Catholic. He liked movies, running, reading, wine-tasting. His favorite spot was in his back yard by his fire pit. I checked his photos. He had an easy smile. One photo with the Lakeside Running Club sign, one at a Habitat site in a hard hat (cute, annoyingly), and one dancing with his daughter at what had to be her wedding.

I read his message:

Michael M-Lakeside:
Hello Renee.
I am Michael, but you can call me Mike. That's what my friends call me and I hope we can be friends.
We seem to have a lot in common, except that I have a cat and not a dog- but I do love dogs. I got the cat when my son moved in with his girlfriend- she was allergic. Plus, I travel quite a bit for work, and cats are self-sufficient.

I'm also a runner. I am a co-founder of a running club here in Lakeside. We have about 20 members. It's really just a lot of older guys like me trying to stay in shape. We run three miles on the trails around the lake, then go have coffee. They are a great bunch of people. Maybe you could come sometime.

I would love to meet you in person. Maybe we could meet for coffee or a glass of wine. See what happens. Maybe we make a new friend, maybe we fall in love. 🙂

I hope you will.

All the best
Mike

I looked at his photos again. I re-read his profile, looking for anything, something that might possibly be a red flag. I read the message again. It was cute. I laughed softly at the last line. *Maybe we fall in love?*

I smiled despite myself. Maybe we do.

I didn't even call Amy to ask her opinion. I just texted her to let her know that I was going to agree to meet MichaelM-Lakeside. She replied with an "All clear."

ReneeM-Den:

Hi Mike.

Thank you for your message. I enjoyed it. I would love to meet you sometime. Here is my number.
I left my number, and clicked send.

Later that evening, I had a call from an unknown number.

"This is Renee"

"Renee. Hi. This is Mike. From Date4U." He was tentative. Michael was the most popular boy name in the mid to late 70's. I am sure plenty of people ask "Which Mike?" I didn't know any other Mike's.

"Mike, Hi. It's nice to hear from you."

"Thank you for sharing your number with me. And Happy Mother's Day. "

"Thanks."

"How was your day?"

We launched into easy conversation. It started with my Mother's Day, which easily segued to children. He also had a son and a daughter. They were both just a year or so older than mine. His daughter was married, and they were expecting their first child. It was easy and genuine; the kind of conversation that made time disappear.

"Would you like to meet for coffee sometime?" He asked.

"Yes, I would like that." I replied. And I would.

We made plans to meet for coffee at 10 on Tuesday. I had a dentist appointment at 11:30 near the coffee shop and had taken the half day off. Mike happened to be in town, and as a sales rep had a flexible schedule.

I was nervous as I dressed. I wanted to make a good impression, so I chose something that was both comfortable but also that made me feel my best.

Mike and I arrived almost at the same time and met in the parking lot. We walked to the shop, and he held open the door for me. Mike is 6'2", casually put-together- jeans, a blue striped button-down, sleeves rolled. His cologne was clean and quiet. We talked for an hour that vanished in ten minutes, and I was annoyed at my dentist for existing.

As we walked to the lot, Mike asked, "May I see you again?

"Yes, I would like that." I replied.

He smiled broadly. "I will call you then."

I was having a margarita with Amy when Mike sent me a text thanking me for meeting him for coffee, and telling me how much he enjoyed meeting me. I read it and beamed. Amy noticed.

"Who is that?" she asked.

"Mike M." I smiled. Then told her all about it.

"Wow! He really made quite an impression on you."

He certainly had.

◆ ◆ ◆

Mike and I spoke and texted a few times over the week. We had made plans to have dinner Friday night.

Amy and I had a strict rule about not sharing an address until the third date, so I met Mike at the restaurant- a cute little Italian place that was BYOB. He greeted me with a kiss on the cheek and we sat down. We easily launched into conversation.

About half way through dinner as we were talking, Mike gently placed his hand on the table- a silent invitation for me to hold it. I placed my hand in his without any hesitation. As we continued to talk, he made lazy circles on the back of my hand with his thumb. The way my hand felt tiny in his, the warmth of his touch- it all felt natural, like we'd done this a hundred times before.

Walking to my car after dinner, Mike laced his fingers through mine, he pulled my hand to his lips and gently placed a kiss on the back of my hand. His grip was warm and easy, like it had always been meant to be there. Holding hands with him didn't feel like a gesture—it felt like belonging. Like I was being claimed in the gentlest way, not with pressure, but with presence. Like he was choosing me.

The night was beautiful- soft air, clear skies, and maybe a tiny flicker of hope that something real had just begun.

We got to my car, and neither of us spoke. Mike reached up and tucked a hair behind my ear, and without a word or hesitation, he leaned in and kissed me. His kiss was soft. I leaned into him and the kiss deepened.

I didn't think. I just felt. I felt his arms around me, his soft lips against me, the beat of his heart. The beat of mine. It nearly stole my breath.

He pulled back and whispered "Good night."

He opened my car door for me, and closed it once I was seated. I watched him walk to his car.

Wow!

◆ ◆ ◆

Once my brain reconnected with my body, I pulled out of the parking lot and called Amy. It was a little after 10, but I didn't care. This was an emergency. I needed to gush.

She picked up with a suspiciously cheerful, "Sooo…?"

"Oh my *gosh*, Amy! It was *so* great. I forgot how good a *good* kiss could be." I was willing to invest in an entire new shoe collection if I couldn't get my toes to uncurl. It was worth it.

"Sounds like you're gonna need a visit from BOB tonight," she said, deadpan.

"Wait—what?"

"You know—BOB. Battery Operated Boyfriend." She giggled like she'd just invented the term.

"Oh my God, Amy. That's disgusting."

I couldn't help thinking that might not be out of the question.

Not that I'd ever admit that to her. Or *anyone*.

She snorted. "Are you seeing him again?"

"Yes. He invited me to run with his running group tomorrow morning."

"'Run.' Is that code for S-E-X?" I swear, Amy could turn a weather report into foreplay.

"I'm hanging up now."

"Okay. Love you. Proud of you. Stay hydrated."

"Love you too."

The next morning, I met Mike in Lakeside. We ran the trail together, the rhythm of our steps falling into an easy cadence. Mike occasionally slowed to pull me aside for a kiss- sexier and more playful today than before. I was enjoying every one of them, the warmth and attention stirring something inside me.

Still, there was a small, quiet voice at the back of my mind- a flicker of doubt I couldn't quite name. Everything felt good, but not quite everything I thought it might. I pushed the thought aside, choosing instead to savor the moment.

After the run, I went home and he headed out for coffee, but not before we made plans to catch a movie later that evening.

I considered it our fourth date, so I gave Mike my address. He picked me up to go to a movie.

I did a quick clean of the house. I played some light jazz, and was putting away the vacuum when Mike rang the doorbell.

Prince ran to the door like he always did. When I opened the door, Prince dropped low, the hair on the back of his neck rising. A low, deep growl rumbled from him- a clear warning. He looked ready to spring, his predatory instincts on high alert. I couldn't imagine what set him off.

Mike walked in, and gave me a quick kiss. Prince jumped on him, and was barking loudly, the fur on his neck was standing.

I pulled my dog off of him "I am so sorry. He has never done that before."

Mike seemed to laugh it off. "It's OK. I'm a stranger."

"Please make yourself at home. I am just going to put him in his crate and we can go."

I put Prince in his crate, and returned to the living room. Mike was leaned back, one hand over the back of the sofa, and his ankle on his knee. He looked comfortable.

"I am really sorry about that. He didn't bite you, did he?"

"No, no, I'm fine." He said. "It's ok."

We left. We watched a light comedy, and shared popcorn. The theater seats were like recliners with large armrests and drink holders, so there was no cuddling, but Mike was never far-holding my hand, or resting a hand on my leg.

We got home, and he walked me to the door. He left me breathless again with another toe-curling good night kiss.

And so, it went for Mike and I. We saw each other a few times a week, texted daily, talked occasionally. He was "just right", attentive without being too clingy. Communicative without being a nuisance. Affectionate without being suffocating.

Mike hosted a barbecue every year for Memorial Day. He'd served in the military before college-A proud veteran, he was very patriotic. Of course, he invited me. The barbecue was at 3 on Saturday of Memorial Day weekend.

I rang Mike's doorbell with a tray of baked beans in my hands. He greeted me with a kiss and took the beans to the kitchen. He fixed me a soda, and we walked into the back yard- already buzzing with light chatter from the friends who were there.

We walked around, and he introduced me. One or two of them looked at me curiously, and seemed to be a little uncomfortable. I also thought it was odd that Mike only referred to me as Renee, and didn't clarify our relationship. Like- *This is my friend Renee, my girlfriend Renee, my date Renee*- Something to give people context.

I assumed I was his girlfriend. I was still new to this stuff. Maybe that wasn't appropriate yet. Maybe he was being considerate by not putting a label on it when we hadn't discussed it.

He was also a little standoffish. He didn't put his hand on my back or hold my hand as we walked around the yard.

A woman walked into the back yard. She was pretty, and about my age. Mike was standing beside me, and he froze when he saw her. She smiled and walked towards us.

"I'll be right back." He said to me, and walked quickly toward her. "You came!" he called to her, sounding more shocked than delighted.

Something about this was off. I looked over and a couple of Mike's friends were huddled in a corner looking from me to them and snickering.

It was a running joke in my family, that my intuition was as close to clairvoyance as one could get as a catholic- Catholics didn't believe in that stuff. Unfortunately, my intuition was popping off like a machine gun. And if it walks like a duck and talks like a duck, it's likely a stupid duck man who must have invited more than one girlfriend to his barbecue.

He walked his possible other girlfriend into the house. Maybe I was over-reacting. I didn't know that he invited another girlfriend. She could be a friend. She could be married. Maybe a work associate. I decided to go inside and introduce myself-away from prying eyes.

I walked in the back door and had not made it to the kitchen, but still had a front row seat to my humiliation- Mike and the new woman- he had his hand on the small of her back, and he leaned down and kissed her.

Mike didn't see me at first. When he finally did, I could see the blood drain from his face.

I turned and walked out the front door. He could keep the Pyrex. He could choke on the beans. I was out.

"Renee, wait. Please, Renee." Mike had come out of the house after me. "Let me explain."

I wasn't looking back.

By the time I reached my car, he'd caught up with me. I'd opened the door, when he placed a hand on my shoulder.

"Please Renee, let me explain."

I turned and silently faced him. I was wearing my Momface now- the one that said "this had better be good, or you are grounded for life." I think he was a little scared, he backed up ever so slightly.

"I met Kim before I met you. We went out once or twice. I forgot I told her about the barbecue. I was so surprised when she showed up. I was going to explain to her that I was seeing someone, I just hadn't gotten to it." He explained.

The problem was, I didn't completely believe him. Something about kissing her in his kitchen while I was out in the back yard. Not acceptable.

"Good bye, Mike." I got in my car.

I sat for a minute and sighed. Dating was supposed to get easier with age, right? Clearly, my man picker needed serious recalibration. I wondered if they had repair shops for that.

I looked up and started the car. I checked my rear-view mirror before I pulled away, and saw Kim stomping away, Mike on her heels. Served him right.

I headed home.

"Hey Siri, text Amy"

"What do you want to say to Favorite Sister"

"Code Pink."

Amy met me at my house, and had the Pink Panty Dropper makings with her. I had pulled out the pitcher she gave me for Christmas, and we mixed them up. We carried the drinks and the pitcher to the back patio.

"Cheers" we toasted and sipped.

After a few quiet moments, I told Amy everything that happened. I needed to say it out loud- needed someone else to witness the humiliation and feel my anger just long enough so I could let it go.

And I did.

I didn't waste another thought on Mike. I'd finally learned how to cut my losses without looking back.

Before I went to bed, I placed my phone on the charger. I noticed several missed calls, voice mail, and texts from MIke. I deleted them all without bothering to read or listen. I blocked his number.

I slept like a baby.

CHAPTER 24

Scott and Ashley were getting married today.

I had found the perfect wedding guest dress- a blush-colored halter, sheer chiffon floating over soft silk. The hemline dipped from just above my knees in front to a graceful sweep at my ankles in back. My cream-colored strappy sandals had tiny blush flowers stitched over the toes- delicate and a little whimsical. I carried a matching clutch and finished the look with dainty pearl drop earrings...and the bracelet David gave me for Christmas.

I had RSVP'd with a plus one. At the time, I was hopeful—hedging a quiet bet that maybe Mike would be the one to go with me. But that morning, as I got dressed alone, I realized I was perfectly at peace.

It felt like freedom.

Somewhere along the way, I had stopped measuring my worth by whether or not I had someone beside me. I had learned to enjoy my own company, to trust myself, to feel whole. Not because I'd given up on love—but because I finally understood: real love doesn't come from needing someone to fill a space. It comes from two whole people choosing to walk beside each other.

And I was ready for that, whenever it happened.

I found my friends- David, Disha, Lonnie and his wife Sue, Pete and his wife Kathy- all seated in the same row. When I saw David was alone, I felt a flicker of relief. And then, just as quickly, guilt.

I had wanted David. And I had wanted David to want me. That's why I didn't speak up that night after the Christmas dinner- not because I was afraid, but because I needed him to choose me. I needed him to prove something I hadn't yet learned to believe for myself.

But I did now.

That need- the aching want to be chosen- had softened into something sturdier. I no longer needed to be wanted to feel worthy. I was enough, on my own. And I understood now: the right person would choose me without hesitation, and I would choose them. It would be simple. Mutual. Like Ashley and Scott. No guessing. No games. Just ease.

The ceremony was beautiful. Ashley was a stunning bride. Afterward, the preacher invited guests outside for cocktails while the wedding party stayed for photos. As we started to walk out, he called for the Denton Running Walking Club to remain for pictures. We all sat back down, surprised and smiling.

The photographer called us up first. We hugged Scott and Ashley. "I'm so glad you all came." Ashley said. "Scott and I never would've met if it weren't for you guys."

Disha and I shared a look. We didn't need to say anything.

Pictures taken, the run club group walked out together and made our way to the patio, where tables were set with centerpieces of peonies, roses, and baby's breath in glass vases. There were twinkle lights overhead and a view of the glistening lake. I found our table and sat with David, Disha, and the rest of the group. Cocktail hour breezed by with laughter and shared memories.

A buffet dinner was served, after which wait staff poured champagne for everyone. There were many toasts, tears, and cake. The whole affair was a beautiful tribute to love, friends, and family.

That's what marriage is, right? It's not just two people coming together—it's all the friends and family who loved and supported them as individuals, now loving and supporting them as a couple- for better or worse, in sickness and in health.

By the end of dinner, I had just about felt all the feelings a person could manage in one night. So, when the band struck up "24 Karat Magic," it felt like a lifeline back to the surface. And true to form, David was the first to jump up- pulling me and Disha with him. I didn't resist.

The bass thumped through the floor, and the whole crowd moved with it — glittering dresses, loosened ties, clinking glasses. At first, it was just fun: laughing with Disha, spinning under David's arm, singing along to every word. But somewhere between the chorus and the bridge, the noise around us blurred. The voices, the music, even the light- it all seemed to dim until there was only him.

We moved like we'd been dancing together for years, each step easy, instinctive. When he looked down at me and smiled, something in my chest gave way. For a long, dizzy moment, I forgot there was anyone else in the room.

And that was when I realized — this is what I wanted. *He* is who I wanted. I'd wasted too much time afraid to go after what I wanted. Tonight, I was done with that.

After the send-off, David guided me toward the parking lot, his hand on the small of my back - steady, easy. He walked beside me and took my shoes to carry for me.

I realized it was time. I had carried this question for so long. I was ready for the answer now. No matter what it was. I knew it wouldn't break me.

I stopped and turned to face him.

"I want to ask you something. And I want you to be completely honest. There's no wrong answer."

"Okay," he said cautiously.

"Why not me?"

"Why not you, what?"

"Why haven't you ever considered me as someone you might be with?"

Just saying it out loud lifted something heavy from me.

"Renee," he said, quiet. "What makes you think I haven't?"

I blinked.

"So, you *have* thought about it," I said, more statement than question. "And... you weren't interested."

"I didn't say that."

He paused. Closed his eyes like he was finding the right words.

"Renee, I've always wanted to be with you. From the first day I saw you at run club- maybe even from the *first* time I saw you. At the courthouse.

When something good happens, you're the first person I want to tell. When something bad happens, same thing. You're my first thought in the morning, my last one at night. I want to run every mile beside you. I want to dance every dance with you. You're my best friend."

My breath caught.

"Then why didn't you say something?"

"I tried," he said, almost smiling. "But you told me you weren't ready."

I remembered that night at run club, the easy miles, the casual question that didn't feel so casual now. "That was an excuse," I admitted quietly. "Maybe I wasn't ready or maybe I was afraid."

He nodded. "Maybe I wasn't really ready then, either. The truth is... I was afraid. Afraid of messing up what we already had. You're too important to me, and I didn't want to lose you. I wasn't sure you felt the same."

A warm breeze stirred, carrying the hum of cicadas from somewhere beyond the twinkling lights strung over the lot. We stood there, eyes locked, not moving, not speaking — each of us waiting to see what the other would do next.

" But I'm not afraid now."

Then he stepped in and kissed me. A gentle, questioning kiss. Testing the water.

He pulled back, waited. Looked at me — his eyes telling me everything I needed to know.

In that moment, *I knew.*

I knew this would be the last first kiss I would ever have.

Everything in me stilled.

All I could hear was my racing heart. All I could see was David, looking at me. His words, his kiss, his eyes all giving me the same answer.

We'd made a choice.

Then- like something in both of us snapped- we reached for each other at the same time. Our lips collided, the kiss urgent, needy, and breathless. It was like something inside of me came undone- like everything I'd been pushing down- every feeling I'd tucked behind polite smiles and cautious distance- rushed to the surface all at once.

There was no hesitation, no pretense. Just need. His arms wrapped around me, pulling me in like he'd been waiting just as long, just as quietly, just as hopefully. My hands found his shoulders, his jaw, his hair- I couldn't touch enough of him, couldn't be close enough. Every part of me leaned in, leaned forward, leaned home.

We stepped into what was always waiting, what was inevitable.

"I knew it!" Disha's voice rang out. "Ha! I won!"

We turned. Disha grinned and held out her hand. Pete groaned and slapped a twenty into her palm.

"She's been running a whole prediction pool since the Halloween run. Ashley had February. I had October. Disha had June."

"Don't complain, Pete. You got the water bottle for entering the pool."

"The *what*?" I asked.

"I got some sponsors and had some water bottles made. They say *'Love's not a dash - it's a distance run.'*" Disha beamed proudly.

David looked at me, "Our love story is a sponsored event."

I looked at David- and we both burst out laughing.

Our friends waved bye as they walked away.

I looked at David, my David. My best friend. My support. My love.

"Let's get out of here before someone else tries to sponsor us.".

EPILOGUE

I was hosting Pie Wednesday this year. Normally, I might worry that my house was too small for the crowd we were expecting, but the unseasonally warm weather made it easy—perfect for a fire in the firepit and plenty of outdoor seating. Worst case, we could stick a few guests in the garage with folding chairs and call it "rustic charm."

It wasn't David's year to have Simon for the week, but he and his ex-wife, Karen, had worked out a better shared custody arrangement. David would be bringing Simon over tonight and returning him to Karen in the morning. They had even managed to carve out more time with Simon during Christmas.

David and I had agreed to skip the Turkey Trot this year. Instead, we planned to have coffee and cinnamon rolls while watching the parade with Prince- because nothing says "holiday fitness" like frosting and marching bands.

I had some ideas about other ways we might burn off those calories.

David and Simon arrived around four to help me set up. We'd taken our time carefully weaving me into Simon's life, determined to set a good example of what a healthy, respectful relationship looked like. We were both lucky to have parents who modeled that for us, and we wanted Simon to have the same.

We never talked about our past relationships or dating lives once we finally got together. None of those people mattered anymore. Every awkward coffee date, every "it's not you, it's me" text, every moment of doubt had simply led us here. We were runners, after all- always focused on the road ahead... though occasionally stopping for snacks.

A few hours later, Pie Wednesday was in full swing. I took a quiet moment to soak in all that had happened in the past year and to appreciate the blessings around me- the people I loved most.

Aaron and Katie, her diamond engagement ring catching the firelight, sat by the firepit with Disha and the run club crew. Ashley, starting to show a little baby bump, was glowing as she shared stories about the months ahead. My baby Morgan tossed a ball to Prince, who wagged his tail like it was his job. Mattie and Simon were playing cards on the floor, their laughter drifting up between shouts of "no fair!" My parents and Sharon were deep in conversation with Tim- Dad and Tim animatedly debating this year's Cowboys as if the outcome depended on their personal input. Amy was in the kitchen, working on pies alongside my love, David- who was wearing the frilliest apron I could find, complete with ruffles that could've doubled as satellite dishes.

This- this was the best new normal I could have ever imagined.

DEBORAH KEDZIERSKI

ABOUT THE AUTHOR

Deborah Kedzierski

Deborah Kedzierski writes contemporary women's fiction with humor, heart, and a dash of real-life awkwardness. Her debut novel, A New Normal Life, was inspired by the twists, turns, and unexpected joys of starting over. When she's not writing, she enjoys spending time with her family, spoiling her dog, or creating something crafty. She lives in Texas.

www.deborah-kedzierski.com

RECIPE FOR PINK PANTY DROPPERS

Pink Panty Droppers

My sister introduced me to the drink she called a *Pink Panty Pulldown.* That was a lot to remember after I had one or two, so I called them *Pink Panty Droppers.*

I researched the recipe, and it's actually called *Pink Lemonade Punch.*

You can make this in a pitcher or - in a pinch, try a large bowl.

1 Liter bottle of Fresca

1 6 oz can pink lemonade

6 oz Vodka

Mix together. Serve over ice.

ACKNOWLEDGEMENT

I am remarkably blessed, and I have so many people to thank for their support during the writing. publishing and promoting of this book. I am overwhelmed by all of the kind words and support I have received from friends and family alike.

Special thanks goes out to my granddaughter, Harper, for the cover art for the book.

Also, to my dog, Tanner for inspiring me to include a dog in the story.

Thank you to Dana Hiser who did the beta reading and editing. The story is much improved thanks to Dana's feedback.

www.ingramcontent.com/pod-product-compliance
Lightning Source LLC
Chambersburg PA
CBHW021037130626
46552CB00005B/1892